He felt so g

Libby's lips were playing at Holt's ear as her hands roamed over his bare shoulders. His response was explosive—her buttons flew as he stripped off her blouse. Libby laughed, a husky, seductive sound.

"You know exactly how to get to me, don't you?" Holt groaned. Desire shone from his blue eyes as he looked at her, and the wave of emotion coursing through her took away her breath.

"Too much..." she breathed. "It's as if we're drowning."

His big hands pulled her close, and he hugged her fiercely. "But what a way to go...."

Books by Marion Smith Collins

HARLEQUIN TEMPTATION
5—BY MUTUAL CONSENT
22—BY ANY OTHER NAME
35—THIS THING CALLED LOVE
49—ON THE SAFE SIDE
63—THIS TIME, THIS MOMENT
86—WITHOUT A HITCH

HARLEQUIN ROMANCE
writing as Marion Smith
2598—THE BEACHCOMBER

These books may be available at your local bookseller.

Don't miss any of our special offers. Write to us at the following address for information on our newest releases.

Harlequin Reader Service
P.O. Box 52040, Phoenix, AZ 85072-2040
Canadian address: P.O. Box 2800, Postal Station A,
5170 Yonge St., Willowdale, Ont. M2N 6J3

Without a Hitch

MARION SMITH COLLINS

Harlequin Books

TORONTO • NEW YORK • LONDON
AMSTERDAM • PARIS • SYDNEY • HAMBURG
STOCKHOLM • ATHENS • TOKYO • MILAN

With love to our friends
Rita and Barker David,
for all the fun through all the years.

Published December 1985

ISBN 0-373-25186-6

Copyright © 1985 by Marion Smith Collins. All rights reserved.
Philippine copyright 1985. Australian copyright 1985.
Except for use in any review, the reproduction or utilization of
this work in whole or in part in any form by any electronic,
mechanical or other means, now known or hereafter invented,
including xerography, photocopying and recording, or in any
information storage or retrieval system, is forbidden without
the permission of the publisher, Harlequin Enterprises Limited,
225 Duncan Mill Road, Don Mills, Ontario, Canada M3B 3K9.

All the characters in this book have no existence outside the
imagination of the author and have no relation whatsoever to
anyone bearing the same name or names. They are not even
distantly inspired by any individual known or unknown to the
author, and all incidents are pure invention.

The Harlequin trademarks, consisting of the words, TEMPTATION,
HARLEQUIN TEMPTATION, HARLEQUIN TEMPTATIONS,
and the portrayal of a Harlequin, are trademarks of Harlequin Enterprises
Limited; the portrayal of a Harlequin is registered in the United
States Patent and Trademark Office and in the Canada Trade
Marks Office.

Printed in Canada

1

HOLT SIGHED, but the sound was absorbed into the noise of the van's engine and the quiet purr of the television set. His eyes narrowed against the sun's winter glare and against a feeling—totally unfamiliar to him—a feeling akin to helplessness.

He glanced over his shoulder. The person on the long bench seat behind him sat straight, hands folded neatly in her lap, her eyes—those eyes that over the past few days had reflected the wariness in his own—fixed obediently on the tiny flickering screen. He returned his attention to the road that stretched before him for what seemed to be innumerable miles.

Maybe this trip hadn't been such a good idea, after all. His fingers tightened briefly around the wheel in a gesture of frustration, then relaxed again.

Frustration was also an unusual emotion for Holt Whitney to experience when dealing with a member of the opposite sex, no matter what her age. On the contrary, he enjoyed what was, to him, a surprising amount of success with women. He shifted in the contoured seat. All that was behind him now, he reminded himself sternly. He would have to use the knowledge and information he had carefully gathered, instead of instinct, to cope with this particular female. She baffled him.

His gaze flickered to the left to check the side mirror, and his spirits lifted as he grinned at the sight framed there. A small sporty car was passing him. Now that one he could probably handle, he thought with a soft chuckle.

The young woman was singing at the top of her lungs. At least he presumed that was what she was doing. He couldn't hear, of course, but her fingers were tapping out a rhythm on her steering wheel and her mouth was open. For the first time he appreciated riding in a vehicle that had a height advantage over the average car. Truck drivers must have a ball.

She was pretty. Her head was tilted to one side, her lips moving, which screwed up her face in a comical expression that didn't detract at all from her features. Her eyes were hidden by oversize sunglasses, but her nose was straight and slightly upturned. The curve of her cheek and jaw were decidedly feminine, and her lower lip was generous and full. Tempting. Her hair fell around her shoulders like a wealth of spun gold. Holt had always had a weakness for blondes.

Suddenly she met his eyes. Her mouth snapped shut, and he could almost feel her embarrassment. The small car accelerated sharply to pass his van.

The grin lingered on Holt's face, but already his mind was returning to that person in the back seat. Hell! Why was he even speculating on another woman? This one would occupy all his energy and concentration for some time to come. Still, old habits were hard to break. He hit the horn lightly with the heel of his hand.

LIBBY HAMILTON TAPPED HER LEFT TOE in rhythm to the upbeat song coming from the radio as she pulled into the passing lane. Her singing was exuberant, a perfect match for her spirits. The new car, the wonderful smell pleasing her senses, handled like a dream.

Brave December sunlight poured in through the windshield, its warmth a kiss on her fingers. Her heart beat with light feathery strokes of happiness and anticipation. She enjoyed the unfamiliar sensation of her hair brushing her shoulders. Normally the thick mane was confined in a practical twist appropriate to a serious-minded computer expert. She inclined her head and opened her mouth to continue the second line of the chorus. Abruptly her lips clamped shut.

The man in the van she was passing had caught her attention. He was laughing at her.

She returned her gray eyes to the road and increased the pressure on the gas pedal until she was out of his line of vision, then shrugged. This wasn't the old Libby Hamilton. What did she care for the opinion of a total stranger? A frown of embarrassment at being caught doing something so undignified, evolved into a reluctant smile before disappearing like a puff of smoke. Today was her day, tailor-made.

Chuckling to herself, she picked up the song on the second verse. When she regained the right-hand lane, in front of the van, she could see the man's face, still smiling, in her mirror.

He hit his horn lightly, in salute, and she forgave him for laughing. She toyed with the idea of waving back, but dismissed it as he increased his speed to stay behind her. After twenty-seven years of parental reminders and warnings, experience still dictated a certain amount of caution.

He had a nice face, Libby decided, when she realized he wasn't going to play a passing game with her. She removed the dark glasses that sat on her nose and settled them on top of her head. Seeing him for the first time without an amber filter, she amended her original observation. That face was more than nice.

The man was handsome without being perfect. Broad intelligent forehead, square jaw, smiling eyes— he was a particularly suitable example of masculinity. When he'd smiled, his white teeth had been in startling contrast to a deep tan. Surprising. Not many people in Illinois kept their tans into December.

But she wasn't in Illinois. The Indiana Welcome Station was only a memory. She was well under way on the first leg of her journey to a new home, a new job— a spectacular job—a new life.

Not that the old life had been all that bad—she admitted in reaction to the small prod of guilt—just stifling. A large loving family could sometimes smother its youngest member without design and with all the best intentions.

Her looks were the culprit. If people would only realize that a serious soul dwelled in this rather lush body, her brothers and sisters wouldn't have felt they had to protect her, and her parents wouldn't have tried to live in her pocket. To them the only successful daughter was a married daughter. She had fought against the growing resentment and bitterness, done everything possible to reinforce the image of what she was, an earnest, solemn, career-oriented woman. But none of her efforts had any effect.

Those days were over for good. That sparkling, goose-pimply feeling that always accompanied an exciting adventure shot through Libby. She hummed along with the radio and, for lack of anything else to do, further contemplated the man in the mirror.

His large hands maneuvered the oversize steering wheel with confident ease. The color of his eyes wasn't discernible from this distance, but they looked to be at least as dark as his hair. She could tell he was alone in the van from the silhouette of the empty seat beside him.

The van itself was questionable—shiny new, but a rather nauseating shade of puce, with white and black stripes—much too gaudy for her taste. He hadn't looked like the sort who would like puce, either.

Road games, played as a child on long boring rides, came back to her, and since there was nothing else to distract her, she indulged herself....

The man was probably a van salesman, delivering— Her thoughts veered to another track, an even better one. He was a rock star on his way to join his group in Indianapolis. They all wore puce costumes, threw roses to screaming teenagers and burned their guitars at the end of each performance.

She grinned at the mental picture. What did they call themselves? Wine on the Moon? Purple Punks? No, this one definitely didn't look punky. Purple Hunks would be more descriptive.

But the van wasn't *exactly* purple. It was closer to the shade of baloney that had been left unwrapped in the

refrigerator for a week or so, just before the mold began to sprout.

Baloney Maloney. That was a good name—just the
right amount of whimsy to indicate the band didn't take
itself too seriously.

Baloney Maloney must be fairly successful. Accord-
ing to her brother, those fancy vans were expensive.
The vertical windows were shaded with horizontal
blinds of the kind that could be tilted against the sun's
glare. A chrome ladder climbed one of the back doors,
and the vinyl cover for the extra wheel proclaimed this
was a custom van from Ad-VAN-tage in Chicago, Illinois.

Libby blinked, realizing he had passed her. She was
looking once more at the back of the vehicle. She shook
her head. She had better concentrate on her driving and
forget the road games and the man in the van.

WHEN LIBBY REACHED THE NORTHERN PERIMETER of Indianapolis, she began to look for a service station that
would accept her credit card. The gas gauge of her
compact didn't read empty, but she'd promised her father never to let it get below a quarter of a tank. No
point in breaking parental promises on the first day out.

Libby smiled ruefully. She remembered saying that
very thing to herself five years ago when she'd graduated from college and moved from her parents' home
to her own apartment. She should have known that two
brothers and their wives, two sisters and their hus-
bands, and two parents, would be more efficient than
the Chicago Police Department at keeping tabs on her.

It had taken her a year or more to realize they were allowing her only the illusion of independence. One or the other of them was always dropping in on her, armed with a flimsy excuse.

And her dates... If one didn't happen to be, for instance, a neighbor's sister-in-law's cousin's son, he came under immediate suspicion, and if he asked her out more than twice, her family assumed it was time to reserve the church. The poor man had to be strong to stand up under that kind of parental and sibling inquisition.

Apparently enough of them had thought she was worth her family's suspicious questioning, because she never lacked for companionship. But if they didn't mind, Libby did.

She suddenly thought of Dan, and the memory brought a wash of guilt. Dan was a dear friend, handpicked by her oldest brother to be more. She had thought herself in love when they became engaged, but had soon realized her mistake when Dan had wanted her to account for every minute of her time. His assumption that she would give up her career when they married made her realize bitterly that Dan would be just an extension of her family.

She knew that she was independent and capable, but she had finally faced the fact that her family would never release the bonds of love as long as she lived nearby.

Libby adored them—it was a wrench to leave—but she had fought for this space. They would have a long way to travel if they intended to monitor her movements in Florida. And she doubted that the computer center that operated all of TOLTOT would be as easy to infiltrate as the business in Chicago had been. Her oldest brother had just happened to know the manager there.

The familiar oil-company logo finally appeared on outlandish stilts in the distance. With a smooth, competent twist of her wrists, Libby took the next exit ramp.

TOLTOT, an acronym for Today's Link to Tomorrow, was a futuristic theme park in south-central Florida, and Libby's destination. Or it would be on January 2. Today was the eighteenth of December. She had allowed herself a couple of weeks to find a place to live.

And the ruckus that had caused! "You won't be home for Christmas?" her mother had exclaimed, exactly as though Libby had plunged a knife into her heart. Her daughter admitted to a certain amount of regret that she would be spending Christmas alone, but she squelched the feeling with the same determination that was the hallmark of the new, liberated Libby Hamilton.

THE GASOLINE PUMPS were situated in front of a large and busy truck stop. She maneuvered her midget among the giants, slightly intimidated by the size of the monstrous vehicles.

An attendant, bundled up in a down jacket and earmuffs, came out of the building with a lazy jog once she had switched off the motor. "Fill it up, please," she said, climbing from the car. She reached back inside for her coat and purse, decided against the coat and closed the car door.

"Yes, ma'am." His breath was a white puff as he smiled at her, analyzing the figure inside designer jeans and a bulky cable-knit sweater with all the appreciation of a connoisseur.

Libby slung the strap of her large bag over her shoulder and smiled back at the unspoken but obvious compliment in his appraisal. Her long-legged stride took her quickly into the large, low building that housed rest rooms, a cashier's booth, a restaurant—but not before the frigid air had wiped away the comfortable feeling of warmth nurtured by the car heater and the sunshine.

Turning right off a central hallway decorated with loops of silver garland and plastic holly, she saw the door marked Ladies. When she tried the knob she found it was locked. Restlessly she rubbed her arms to stimulate warmth and walked back and forth in the narrow space.

A burly driver gave her an interested smile as he passed her to enter the door marked Gents. It wasn't until he came out a few minutes later that she realized how long she'd been waiting. Maybe the door was just stuck. Once more she reached for the knob, but before she could grasp it, she felt it turn under her fingers.

She stepped aside, waiting for whoever was inside to come out. The door remained closed. Impatient now, she started to knock, when a whimper arrested the action.

"Help. I can't get out." It was a child's voice, a young child if she wasn't mistaken. She took a firm grip on the knob, but the door refused to give.

"Please, help me."

She could hear the hysteria build as the child began to cry. Without further hesitation Libby knocked firmly on the wooden panel. "Sweetheart, don't cry. Listen to me."

She thought the sobs lessened a bit and took advantage to speak in a firm reassuring voice. "Is there a button on the doorknob in there?"

Instead of an answer, the cries rose to a frantic level. Libby looked helplessly down the empty hall. Finally she knocked again. "Sweetheart, I'm going to find someone to open the door. Don't be afraid. I'll be right back to get you out."

There was no response except the frightened sobbing. The sound wrenched her heart. Poor child. She whirled and hurried to the front of the building.

A man in a sheepskin coat was standing at the cashier's cubicle, but she hardly noticed as she brushed past him to speak into the half-moon opening in the glass. "There's a child locked in the ladies' room. Do you have a key?" She ignored the gruff imprecation from the man whose place she had usurped.

"Yes, I'll get it."

Libby blessed the young woman's speed as she swiveled in her chair and whipped a key from a hook behind her. "Do you need help?" she asked, leaning forward as she slid the key through the opening.

"Maybe not," Libby told her. She snatched up the key and hurried back down the hallway.

The man she had pushed in front of was now gripping the flimsy doorknob of the ladies' room with ferocious vigor. In another minute he would wrench the thing off, and their problems would be compounded. "I have a key," she told him.

Instead of moving back, he snatched the key from her fingers. "Thanks," he said curtly, but the word was more condemning than appreciative. Did the idiot man think she'd locked the child in? She bit back a smart retort.

Finally he had the door open, and a tiny whirlwind erupted from the room. To Libby's absolute astonishment, the little girl flew directly toward her. She stooped, her arms spreading automatically to receive the child. The little girl clung to her, sobbing all the while, and Libby's embrace tightened as she looked up into the eyes of the man who drove the fancy van.

He was much more impressive in person. The heavy coat was open, pushed back by hands set at his waist, revealing faded jeans and a navy sweater of some incredibly soft-looking material. Maybe an inch over six feet tall, he had the body of an athlete, broad-shouldered and lean-hipped. His hair was almost black, the color of strong coffee, and styled casually long. His eyes were dark blue, she observed with total irrelevance, like the sky at dawn, just before the sun began to spread its golden glow. The thickness of his lashes gave his eyes the appearance of being darker.

At the moment those eyes that had laughed at Libby's antics earlier on the freeway were oblivious to her. They looked instead at the child in her arms, their color clouded with confusion and a hint of exasperation. He dropped his hands and came down on his haunches beside them. "Jill...honey..."

The sobs had trailed off to hiccuping sighs, but when he spoke the little girl turned away from him, burying her face in Libby's neck. She whimpered again.

Libby slipped her hand under the child's pink, fur-lined coat and stroked the tiny back with a comforting hand. This baby couldn't be more than three years old. Why on earth had he left her alone? Suddenly a suspicion began to grow in her mind. She hadn't seen anyone else in the van when she had passed it on the highway. Of course, the child was very short.

"I only stepped down the hall to pay for the gasoline. But there was a line." The man answered her unspoken accusation. His voice was deep, well modulated, with a trace of a drawl, and under other circumstances it would have had a soothing, calming effect; right now it struck a nerve in her.

She started to speak, but her words faltered at something in his expression, something he wasn't quite able to hide. He looked like a man saddened by a situation he didn't know how to handle. She doubted the feeling was familiar to him. He had radiated assurance and confidence until the child had run to her. Only then had he seemed at a loss.

Libby had to ask the question that hovered on her tongue. "Is this your little girl?"

"Yes," he answered simply, straightening to his full height.

Libby hesitated. After all, this was none of her business. But then she tilted her chin. A hysterical child was anyone's business. "Are you sure?"

"Dammit! Do you think I don't know my own daughter?"

"She doesn't seem to want to go to you." Libby argued stubbornly, stroking the quivering little shoulders. The familiar scent of baby powder and shampoo rose to her nostrils.

The man sighed deeply and massaged the back of his neck in a tired gesture. "I've just been awarded custody of her," he admitted through gritted teeth. "She hasn't seen me for a long time."

Libby could tell he hated to have to explain himself, but short of dragging the child from her arms, which might cause a stir if she resisted, he had no choice but to answer. That he was infuriated with Libby was obvious, and she couldn't really blame him. Still, she had heard many stories of parents kidnapping their own children. "Do you have any proof?"

Anger, pure and unadulterated, blazed from his eyes. He loomed over her crouched figure, his hands clenched impotently at his sides.

Libby couldn't control her involuntary withdrawal from his physical size and strength. She might be getting into an unmanageable situation.

He took a quick step backward, checking his instincts, but his expression was murderous.

Libby relaxed to a degree when he moved away, but kept a wary eye on his face. A muscle jumped in his jaw as another burly truck driver came down the hall toward them.

The trucker's brows went up, but he didn't say anything as he took in the scene. He touched a finger to his cowboy hat, sidestepped Libby and the child in her arms and disappeared into the men's rest room.

"Perhaps you would like to see the judge's order giving me custody?" the van man sneered when they were alone again.

Despite his animosity there was something else there, too. He was definitely on the defensive for some reason, and she remembered that fleeting look of sadness. Making a sudden decision, she stood, holding the child in her arms. "Yes. I think I'd better," she said calmly.

"Hey, wait just a minute. Where do you think you're going?" the man demanded, but Libby thought she detected a trace of fear in his voice. Did he think *she* was going to steal his daughter?

"We'll be in the restaurant." Deliberately she added a playful lilt to her smile and ruffled the child's blond curls. "Maybe Jill would like a glass of milk, and I could certainly use a cup of coffee."

The little girl raised her head tentatively from Libby's shoulder. Her thumb slid into her mouth as her gaze joined Libby's in assessing the man. Any remaining doubts fled when Libby saw the child's eyes. Even wet with tears, their beautiful blue color could only have been inherited from the man who watched them.

"Dammit! You can't just..." He lifted his arms toward them.

At the sound of the angry voice and the abrupt action, the child sought her haven, burrowing her face into Libby's neck. She began to cry again, quietly, and her little arms clung even tighter.

The man ran a frustrated hand through his hair, further rumpling the thickness.

"Look," said Libby, her sympathy for his predicament fully aroused. If he was telling the truth, as he probably was, this whole episode must be maddening to him. "I'm not trying to be difficult," she added appeasingly. "Your little girl is obviously upset. I've had some experience with children. Let me see if I can soothe her."

He searched her face for a long minute. He must have been at least partially satisfied by what he saw there. "It seems I have no choice," he said grudgingly.

"I promise I won't run away with her, though she is a darling." Libby tilted her head to the side and gave him a tentative smile, activating the dimple in her right cheek.

The slightly friendly shift in her demeanor produced a sudden and shocking response. The broad chest expanded as he caught his breath. His eyes widened in surprise, and a brief flame of sexual awareness flared in their midnight depths. His gaze dropped involuntarily to her mouth, igniting a totally unexpected, but intense physical reaction in Libby.

The silence was warm and heavy, falling like a transparent curtain around them, muffling all outside sounds and sending a shiver of expectation, like a ribbon of heat, from her nape down to her spine. She was aware of each nerve in her body, as it sang in response to the stranger's inherent sensuality. Her feet seemed rooted to the spot. She had to make a positive effort not to moisten her lips against the sudden dryness there.

The child, cuddled next to her breast, wiggled at the unconscious tightening of her arms. The motion finally broke the field of the man's fascination, parting the curtain and freeing Libby from his magnetism. She shook her head to clear her mind of the astonishing dreamlike confusion that had clouded her normally clear thoughts.

"I, uh, I have the court order in my van," the man said hastily, as though afraid Libby would turn and run. She was very close to doing just that.

Libby opened her mouth to tell him that was no longer necessary, but he seemed to anticipate her denial. "Please. I want you to see it," he added softly, like a man speaking to a nervous animal. He didn't touch her, but the gentle tone was equally effective as he locked onto her eyes again. "My name is Holt Whitney."

Her emotions still fluctuated uncertainly, but at last she managed to free one hand from under the child's bottom and untangle it from the strap of her purse. She discovered an overwhelming urge to touch this man, even in such an impersonal gesture as a handshake. Wanting the tactile experience of his skin against hers, she held out her hand. "I'm Libby Hamilton."

It was a mistake. She knew as soon as his fingers curled around her hand that it was a huge mistake. The heat from his firm grip traveled up her arm to her shoulders and swept across them like a warm cloak. He held on to her hand until she tugged, then released it reluctantly.

"I'll take her, um, Jill...?" Was that her voice, thickened to a barely recognizable whisper?

"Yes. Her name is Jill," he affirmed with a distracted nod. He appeared to be as affected as she by the disturbing tension in the air.

"I'll take Jill into the restaurant," she murmured.

"And I'll get the order from my van." He still seemed unwilling to move, to release her gaze. For Libby it was an effort to tear hers away, but she finally managed, by turning her whole body.

As she walked the length of the hall, carrying his daughter, she felt Holt Whitney's eyes on her back. She hoped the unsteadiness in her legs didn't cause her footsteps to waver. Lord! What on earth had happened between one minute and the next to produce a reaction like that? Holt Whitney was one of the most potent men she had ever encountered.

Suddenly she turned. He was standing in the same spot, looking as stunned as she felt. "Will. . ." She stopped to clear her throat. "Will you return the key to the cashier and tell her I'll come back to pay for my gasoline?"

"Sure." He lifted a hand, and she gave him another tentative smile.

"Thanks."

Holt watched her walk away with a feeling akin to relief. Only when the air hit his oxygen-starved lungs did he realize he'd been holding his breath. *There goes one hell of a sexy lady,* he thought dazedly. Her sensuality totally belied the apparently natural reserve that had led her to give him the third degree about his daughter.

He was certainly no stranger to desire, but never had he experienced that gut-twisting hunger so instantaneously. Her eyes...they were unconsciously seductive, the dusky color of smoke, beckoning a man to lose his way into their magical haze. When she'd smiled, when that elusive dimple had winked up at him, the floor had all but fallen from under his feet.

She wasn't tall, maybe five-three or four, but half of that seemed to be legs. In a bathing suit she would be spectacular...in jeans, she wasn't too bad, either. He forced his gaze away from the slight sway of her hips. His gaze met his daughter's over the shoulder of one of the most exciting women he'd ever met.

When he had seen her singing to herself in the car, he had thought she was simply pretty. What an amazing misconception, he thought wryly, watching her move. Maybe it was time to have his eyes checked.

The thick black brows suddenly came together in a frown. Or he should have his head examined, he revised with an inexplicable surge of disappointment. Sighing deeply, he shook his head. *Be practical, Whitney. You don't need this.*

Libby Hamilton was a nice person who had befriended his daughter in a casual if sympathetic way. To use an outdated cliché, they were two ships that pass in the night, two strangers whose lives were touching briefly and then would part, never to merge again. Still...he hadn't imagined her response or the current that had arced between them for a heart-stopping moment.

He turned and took a distracted step, raking his hand through his hair, then turned once more. The key dangled in the doorknob of the door where he'd left it. He yanked it out. God help him, he had enough worry and responsibility right now without mellowing into a romantic, fanciful fool. His long impatient stride carried him back to the cashier's cubicle.

2

WHEN HOLT ENTERED THE RESTAURANT a few minutes later, Libby had settled Jill into a vinyl-covered booth and contrived to soothe both herself and the child into a semblance of calm. She had removed the pink coat and tucked the white ruffled blouse back into matching pink coveralls. Yet, when those distinctive blue eyes looked up at her, she almost panicked. The child had both chubby hands clasped around a glass of milk, sipping between uneven breaths; Libby was endangering her tongue with hasty sips of very hot coffee between bursts of inane chatter. Jill had not uttered a word, but she seemed very content to listen.

"Here's the official document giving me the right to my daughter." Holt tossed the sheaf of papers onto the table and slid into the padded bench opposite them.

Libby glanced up from Jill in surprise. His irritation had returned. She scarcely looked at the blue-backed papers. Instead she studied his face. Bitterness was mixed with the sadness she had seen earlier in his eyes. She understood at once what was bothering him. She set her coffee mug on the table and wrapped both hands around it, in very much the same way Jill held her milk. "Mr. Whitney," she began.

"Holt," he corrected curtly.

"Holt," she acquiesced, searching for the right words. "You said you had only recently received custody of your daughter?" Her finely arched brow rose. She wouldn't fault him if he told her to mind her own damn business.

He nodded. "The day before yesterday. My ex-wife lives in Chicago." He looked first at Jill, then at Libby.

"Then please don't blame Jill for coming to me the way she did," Libby urged with quiet patience. "Perhaps she felt instinctively that I was used to children. Or maybe she's just more accustomed to women than men?"

His instincts were in order, as well, she thought ruefully, as his eyes immediately went to the third finger of her left hand. He frowned. "You have children of your own?"

"No." She chuckled, ignoring the rather blatant disapproval in his voice. "But I have eight nieces and four nephews."

He met her smile with a reluctant grin. "Libby Hamilton comes from a big family, huh?"

"Huge. So, you see, I have had experience."

"Jill is an only child."

"So I gathered," she said dryly. "She won't break, you know."

He let out a long breath and subsided against the back of the seat, relaxing for the first time in the course of the encounter. The heavy jacket hung open, and his slouched posture stretched the sweater tautly across the broad chest. He reached out a finger to give the empty ashtray a careless spin. Then he sat up and rested his elbows on the table edge, building a tower under his chin with his linked fingers.

Libby tried to keep from staring at his mouth as he studied her, concentrating instead on his hands. They were large, well shaped, as tanned as his face, the backs sprinkled with hair, the nails clean and trimmed blunt and short.

His hands looked…capable. Libby wondered… No! Nervously she tucked a strand of her hair behind her ear and met his eyes with what she hoped was an expression of friendly interest.

"In my mind I can tell myself you're right," he said in a low voice. "But in my heart it's hard to rationalize." A knuckle traced the shape of his clean-shaven jaw. "When I realized I really had a chance to gain custody of my daughter…well, I did some studying."

The remark, so revealing, so unashamedly loving, warmed Libby to the tips of her toes.

"Besides, she's so little." His eyes sought his daughter, who was watching him warily. He smiled carefully at her. Lowering both forearms flat on the table, he reached across to tweak his daughter's nose with a gentle finger. "And I love her very much." The child's mouth curved in the beginnings of a smile.

Watching the tender gesture, Libby had to blink back tears herself. Her large family was affectionate, but it was a boisterous kind of affection. This sweet patience was so much more touching.

Suddenly Holt Whitney was much more than a man with tremendous masculine appeal. "That's obvious," she said in a whisper.

He looked at her questioningly for a minute, before crossing his arms on the table in front of him. "I live in Florida. That's why I bought the van," he went on. "It has a refrigerator and a television and a seat that makes into a bed. I thought we'd take our time on the trip, get to know each other."

Evidently he decided not to ask the question that came into his eyes then. Libby wondered what it would have been. She had another thought and tried to hide a smile. "You really are traveling in comfort and style, aren't you? It also has a distinctive color."

Holt laughed; the sound seemed to reach out to her. "You should have seen the one I didn't buy. It had a scene on the side. Sunset over the desert, complete with orange sand and bright-green cacti."

Libby groaned. "I suppose even puce is better than orange sand."

"Unfortunately this miracle of convenience lacks one necessity. And my little Goldilocks has a mind of her own, or maybe a hangover from—what do they call it—the 'terrible twos'?" He widened his smile to show the child that he wasn't really criticizing. "She refused to let me...um..."

"Accompany her into the ladies' room." Laughing, Libby finished the statement for him.

"Exactly." He looked pleased. "She's an independent little thing, isn't she?"

Jill buried her face in the glass.

"Independence is a good character trait to have," Libby said, thinking of her own belated bid for it.

Holt subjected Libby to another long study. "I wouldn't have Jill be any other way," he assured her.

The waitress interrupted at that moment to ask if Holt wanted anything. "Nothing for me, thank you...but maybe the lady would like something? It's almost lunchtime."

"No, thanks. My mother packed me a lunch," she told him wryly, then realized he wouldn't understand the nuance. "My mother's very protective," she explained, drawing another smile from him. "Speaking of lunchtime, I'd really better be on my way."

Libby was surprised and a bit embarrassed at the note of genuine emotion she heard in her own voice when she spoke. This entire incident and her reaction to Holt were unlike her to the point of being baffling. Usually she found it necessary to crush at least a few presumptions in the opening minutes of an encounter with a man, but she felt no such urge with this one. The regret that shaded her tone was born of a feeling that they had somehow skipped a step in their brief acquaintance.

Shaking her head slightly, she reached across Jill for her purse, which was wedged into the corner next to the wall. "I've enjoyed meeting both of you."

"Are you still heading south?"

Without thinking Libby caught her lip between her teeth, hesitant about giving information to this man, who was, after all, a stranger.

Her reluctance was easily readable, and he reacted to it immediately. "Sorry, Libby. I shouldn't have asked. I didn't mean to make you uncomfortable. You know nothing about me, and you're wise to be cautious."

The statement was exactly the reassurance she needed, of course. She half suspected he knew that. She watched him fold and tuck the blue-backed papers into an inside pocket of his jacket. "I doubt that if you had evil designs you would bring your daughter along. Yes, I'm headed south, all the way to TOLTOT."

His brows rose. He seemed pleased with her answer. "On a vacation?"

Without thinking how proprietary the action might look, she took a napkin from the metal dispenser and wiped the milk from the child's upper lip, catching the drop that hovered on her chin. "No, I've accepted a job in the computer center there." She wadded the napkin and dropped it onto the table. Then she scooted out of the booth. "I'm going back to the rest room, Jill. Would you like to go with me?" She accompanied the question with an inquiring glance at Holt.

He gave permission with a nod and a grin. "Thanks."

Jill set her glass down with a determined thump and crawled across the seat.

A few minutes later they were back, Jill clinging to her hand. Holt rose at their approach. Instead of sitting down, Libby drew the child forward with a gentle tug and freed her own fingers. "I've enjoyed meeting both of you. If you ever visit the amusement park, I hope you'll look me up," she said with a deliberate cheerfulness and a wide smile for Jill.

Oh, dear. She hoped the child didn't object with tears when they had to part. Holding her breath, Libby stood aside.

Holt helped Jill into her coat and picked her up.

Jill made no protest this time, but her little body was stiff in Holt's arms and her eyes never left Libby.

Holt pretended to be unaware of his daughter's withdrawal, which propelled him another notch upward in Libby's eyes. He obviously knew he couldn't force things like the love of his child. Moving smoothly, he shifted Jill to one arm, took a look at the check the waitress held out and dug into the pocket of his jeans for a bill. "Thanks," he told the woman, who was about as immune to that devastating grin as Libby had been.

Libby shook off the feeling of envy and preceded them out of the restaurant. She headed for the cashier's cubicle.

"I've already paid for your gasoline," Holt told her. When she opened her mouth to protest, he held up a hand. "It was the least I could do. You probably saved me from an embarrassing scene."

"But I can't accept..."

"Please." His smile was warm. "You've really been a big help."

Jill's legs dangled, front and back, over his hip. She suddenly reached out a small hand to touch Libby's cheek. "Jill thanks you, too." Those were the first words the child had spoken since she'd cried out for help from behind the locked door of the rest room.

Libby caught Jill's hand against her face and turned to plant a loud smacking kiss in the little palm. She grinned. "So Jill really can talk?" she teased, and was rewarded with a smile.

"Okay. Jill can buy my gas." They had reached the entrance, and Libby helped Holt arrange the fur-lined hood carefully over the blond curls and tied the strings under her chin.

"Maybe we'll see you on the road," Holt said as she zipped Jill's jacket. He opened the outside door and indicated with a nod of his head that she should precede him.

Libby turned sideways to edge through the space between his large body and the doorframe. Unfortunately, rather than giving him her back, she was facing him.

The incident couldn't have lasted more than seconds, but this time, when his gaze concentrated on her mouth, the sensation was even more electrifying than before. Then his eyes dropped to her breasts.

Her pulse accelerated dramatically, and she felt her flesh swell against the restriction. She knew that the bulky knit sweater completely hid her shape, but she sensed he could have drawn a picture of her. "Don't do that!" she whispered.

"I'm sorry," he said in that low voice that reminded her of velvet—smooth but slightly prickly. His big hand clasped her shoulder lightly. "I don't mean to embarrass you, Libby. But...I hope you don't take offense...I have to tell you, you're one of the most desirable women I've ever seen." He wore the earnest expression of a man telling the absolute truth.

Libby had learned to control her blushes when she was eighteen, but if the wild hot feeling under her skin was any sign, she was as red as a beet. A quick glance at his face showed he was very much aware of her discomfort, and enjoying it.

Dammit, she raged in silent dismay. Why couldn't he have pretended to misunderstand? The veneer of polite pleasantries that covered potentially embarrassing situations was adequate, if not completely honest. Why couldn't he indulge in them? Irritation at her own predictable response fought with common sense. She wouldn't see this man again. She decided to ignore the compliment, if that's what *he* thought it was, and dropped her chin to scuttle through the door.

What was it he had said earlier? Something about seeing her again? As the cold air hit her she wrapped her arms around her waist, wondering why the improbability of a chance meeting made her shiver more than the biting wind. "Maybe."

"There's no maybe about it," said Holt. "It's true."

"I don't feel comfortable when you say things like that. I meant that maybe we'll see each other on the road," Libby explained firmly. "Goodbye, Jill." She wiggled her fingers at the child and moved in the direction of her car.

The space between them was growing wider with each step, yet she clearly heard the child's husky little voice. "Bye...Libby."

Libby turned to walk backward, her fur-lined boots shuffling across the gravel. She gave them both a pleased smile of surprise and swept her curls away from her face with a hand. "Jill remembered my name." She had to raise her voice to be heard over the air brakes and heavy truck engines.

"You're a pretty unforgettable lady, Libby Hamilton. See you!" he called.

Suddenly his mouth spread in the same kind of outrageous grin she'd first seen several hours ago in his rearview mirror. His gaze was fixed on a point beyond her shoulder. She whirled just in time to keep herself from backing into a gasoline pump.

Watching as the van pulled out of the parking lot, she waved again to Jill, who had her nose pressed to the rear window.

A woebegone tear made its way down her cheek. "Goodbye, Libby," she mouthed.

Holt must have said something. Jill turned her head for a minute, and when she turned back her face was wreathed in a happy smile.

A few minutes later Libby was still wondering what had caused the change when she merged her car into the traffic on the interstate. Whatever the reason for the transformation, she was glad. Jill didn't need tears in her young life; she needed laughter and love.

Without thinking, Libby dialed the radio to a station that was offering ballads instead of soft rock. Holt thought she was desirable.... Dreamily she began to sing along with the love songs.

She hadn't gone more than ten miles when suddenly she sat straight up in her seat and pulled the sunglasses down from the top of her head, pushing them into place with an impatient forefinger. She hadn't checked *his* left hand. Maybe he had remarried.

Frowning, she struggled to remember his hands as he'd sat across the table. The mental picture didn't include a ring, but she wasn't sure she hadn't simply overlooked one. The idea fell on her heart like a weight, sending it plummeting into her stomach.

But no, she rationalized, a man like Holt Whitney probably wouldn't remark on the desirability of one woman if he was married to another.

What did it matter? They were strangers, despite the awareness that had sprung up between them. The odds against their running into each other another time were a million to one, impossibly long. There were hundreds, thousands of people on this highway.

Libby scanned the numbers on the radio dial until she relocated her soft-rock station, but decided it wouldn't hurt her to be on the lookout for a puce-colored van.

SITTING ALL DAY in a car was more exhausting than the most strenuous physical exercise. Libby massaged the back of her neck with her right hand and rotated her head to try to ease the tension.

The plains of Indiana seemed to stretch endlessly on either side of the long straight highway, and the sameness was beginning to dull her responses. What she needed was a cup of coffee to perk her up. The next exit should be about five miles ahead.

Just then she caught sight of two figures huddled together as they walked along the verge of the highway, clearly visible long before she actually reached them. The taller figure, a man, was hunched protectively over the woman. As Libby approached, the woman looked back, turning her body as she did so. She was very pregnant, and her expression was hopeful.

Sympathies aroused, Libby tentatively touched the brake pedal with a booted toe, ignoring every warning about hitchhikers that she'd ever heard. They didn't look dangerous. Maybe their car had just run off the road. Poor thing. She shouldn't be out in this weather at all, much less on a busy road where cars were whizzing by.

Libby passed the two, albeit hesitantly, and as she did the man looked up, too. He was furious. She could read the scowl in the split second when his eyes met hers. For some contrary reason the scowl decided her. It was the expression of a man mad at the world and the conditions that had placed him there.

She braked and signaled her intention to pull off the road a hundred yards or so in front of them. Before she could complete the maneuver, she heard the tap of a horn behind her. Her surprised gaze met Holt's in the rearview mirror.

Now, *that* scowl was aimed directly at her, and so was the anger. He jerked his thumb at a sign in the meadow to their right advertising a coffee shop to be found at the next exit.

She read the information there and looked back to the mirror. The jerk of the thumb was even more definite. He obviously wanted to talk to her.

Resigned, she nodded slightly, her foot returning to the accelerator. The van stayed right behind her. She could no longer see the stranded couple, but she sent them a mental apology.

The exit wasn't far, but the time it took to cover the distance was enough for her to have built up a bit of steam. True, it might be foolhardy to pick up strangers, but what business was it of Holt Whitney's what she did? She wheeled into the drive of the coffee shop and slammed on her brakes. By the time he had parked the van and stepped down, she was out of her car and advancing on him.

She opened her mouth, but before she could get a word out he took the offensive.

"You *fool!*" he snapped, stopping in his tracks and planting his fists on his hips. He was formidable in his anger. "What the hell did you think you were doing?"

"I—"

"Hitchhikers, for God's sake! Have you lost the mind you were born with?"

Libby's chin came up defensively. The cold was beginning to creep in under her sweater. She jammed her hands into the pockets of her jeans and hugged her elbows to her body. "The poor woman was pregnant," she said.

"Maybe. *Maybe* she was pregnant." He sliced the air with his hand. "And maybe that was a pillow stuffed under her dress to get an unsuspecting driver to stop in the middle of nowhere. Worse things have been known to happen. Lady, you're crazy!"

A shiver crossed her shoulders, only partly caused by the weather. She clamped her mouth shut, afraid her annoyance would get the better of her.

Holt had shed his jacket, too. He studied the stubborn thrust of her chin for a moment and sighed deeply. "Get your coat," he said in a moderated tone. "I'll buy you a cup of coffee." He swung back toward the van without waiting for her to answer.

Jill was delighted at the unexpected reunion. She reached for Libby's hand as they entered the coffee shop. "I didn't think Daddy would find you soon, Libby." She let herself be lifted to a bar stool by her father, but all her attention was on her new friend. "We drove and drove."

Libby was too distracted to question the child's wording. "I'm glad to see you again, too, Jill."

"Two coffees," Holt told the woman behind the counter. He settled on the stool on the other side of his daughter. "What do you want, Jill?"

"Coke," said the child. Holt nodded to the woman.

"I'm going back for them," Libby spoke over Jill's head when the drinks were in front of them

"The hell you are," Holt said abruptly.

"Oh-oh. Daddy said a bad word." Jill's singsong brought their gazes to her.

"Sorry," said Holt, tensing the muscle in his jaw to put a hold on his temper. His hand curled around the thick, white mug.

Libby was inordinately pleased to note the absence of a ring and annoyed with herself for the feeling. "The poor woman was pregnant, Holt." She lowered her voice in an attempt to make him understand.

"I know what pregnant means," piped up Jill. "It means when your tummy's fat you've got a baby in there." She patted her own little rounded stomach. "Do you know if I'm pregnant?" she asked Libby innocently.

Both adults swiveled on their stools to stare at her. Finally Holt answered for Libby, who was having a hard time keeping a straight face. "I don't think you're pregnant, sweetheart. You have to be married first." He met Libby's eyes with a grudging smile. "That's the most number of words she's strung together since I picked her up."

"Oh, no, you don't have to be married," Jill disputed. "A friend of Mommy's got pregnant. She said it was a 'damnable nuisance—' " her tongue twisted around the unfamiliar words "—but she didn't have—"

Libby choked on a laugh, and Holt interrupted his daughter. "It's better if you're married," he informed her shortly.

Jill shrugged and returned her attention to her drink.

"Holt, I have to," Libby said quietly. "My conscience won't let me leave them out there."

He inhaled slowly and let out the breath in resignation. "If you'll stay here with Jill, I'll go back to see about them."

"But you—"

"Will you stay with her?" he snapped.

"Yes."

It was more than half an hour before Holt came back and, despite her conviction that the two people were harmless, Libby had just begun to worry. During the few quiet spots in Jill's chatter, she dwelled on the more unpleasant possibilities in the situation. She had sent Holt out on a mission that she thought was one of mercy. But what if he'd been right? What if the couple was dangerous?

When he walked in the door of the coffee shop, she breathed a sigh of relief and smiled. She looked past him for the couple, but he was alone. "Did you find them?"

He nodded. "I took them to the bus station a few miles up the road. They were stone broke, heading for her parents' home in Louisville," he said quietly, gruffly. "Someone had given them a ride partway and then just dumped them."

And you bought their bus tickets, she filled in silently, *so they wouldn't have to hitchhike. Probably gave them money for food, too.* "Thank you, Holt," she said softly.

"We'd better get going." Holt didn't say much more than goodbye as they climbed into their respective vehicles, but Jill called out, "See you tonight, Libby."

Tonight? Still put off by his officiousness, she shrugged. "Bye, Jill."

3

FOR THE PAST FEW MILES, the inevitable signs of what the
Madison Avenue advertisers called civilization had
begun to appear. Thickening traffic, flashy billboards
dressed for the Christmas season and ever-present en-
dorsements of char-broiled, flame-kissed, one-
hundred-percent ground beef vied with Color TV, In-
door Pool, Children Stay Free and Lodging signs.

Grateful at least for the variety in the landscape,
Libby glanced at her watch. She was tired and could see
no reason to press herself to reach her planned destination of Bowling Green, Kentucky. Louisville would
do just as well, she thought as she approached the
bridge over the river that separated Indiana and Kentucky.

A hot bath, a change of clothes and dinner were what
she needed. She could get to bed early and be on the
road in the morning well before the rush hour. Better
yet, she would look for a motel on the other side of
Louisville. Then she could avoid the early-morning
traffic completely.

As the multilane highway wound through the city,
static and interference overcame the radio signal from
Indiana. She twisted the knob. A Louisville station
warned that the weather tomorrow would be overcast

with a chance of snow. Travelers' advisories were out, and she was told to stay tuned to that station for further developments. Drat! Bad weather would slow her progress considerably. She thought fleetingly about trying to push on farther south, but the idea of a bath and a rest won out.

Another billboard informed her that a nationwide chain motel was located at the next exit. She debated her choices. It would be more interesting to get off the main highway, drive around for a while, look for accommodations that weren't the same from San Francisco to Washington, D.C. On the other hand, if the weather was threatening as predicted, she would be better off to stay close to well-traveled roads. Pushing up the wand to activate the blinker signal, she sighed with relief and steered her car into the exit lane.

THE MOTEL ROOM was as colorless as Libby had imagined it would be, but clean and warm. She closed the door and slid the safety chain into its slot. The absolute quiet left her ears ringing after the noise and tension of driving on the interstate.

Dropping suitcase, purse and coat on one bed, she flopped spread-eagled on her back across the other. "Ah..." she breathed aloud as she toed her ankle boots off and let them drop to the carpeted floor. "Just a short nap," she told her mental alarm, and rolled over to pull a pillow from under the spread.

AN HOUR LATER, Libby smiled at her reflection in the mirror and brushed a hint of color high on her cheekbones. She actually felt halfway human again as she ran a brush through her hair until it crackled with winter's electricity. Her hands calmed the static-charged strands back into place.

She had dressed in a pair of soft wool slacks and a matching silk blouse in a shade of sapphire that altered the color of her eyes from gray to smoke. A narrow snakeskin belt defined her small waist, and tan ankle boots raised her height to a respectable five-foot-five. She put on her coat and hooked the strap of her purse over one shoulder.

The temperature seemed to have dropped several degrees since the sun had gone down. Turning up her collar against a chilling wind, she hurried along the concrete strip toward the lobby doors.

A smiling woman holding an armful of menus greeted her beside the garishly decorated Christmas tree stationed at the entrance to the restaurant. "Table for one?" she asked politely.

Libby opened her mouth to answer, but before she could get the words out she felt a tug at the hem of her coat. She looked down into unique blue eyes. "Jill? Where on earth did you come from? What...?"

"Libby, hi," said Jill with a delighted chuckle. "I'm here."

"So am I," drawled a deep voice behind her.

Libby's head swung in amazement; Holt Whitney was at her elbow. She caught her breath. Remembering his mood when they'd parted at the coffee shop, she eyed him warily. "I can't believe this. What a coincidence."

"Not exactly," Holt admitted, leaving her to puzzle out his remark as he turned to the hostess. "A table for three, please." His gaze returned to Libby. "You don't mind, do you?" Electric blue eyes brushed over her in one heated sweep. It was the same kind of inventory he'd subjected her to that morning, just before he'd told her she was desirable. It took her a moment to recover from the effect of his scrutiny.

He mistook her delay for hesitation. "Do you?" he repeated.

What if she did mind? An argument wouldn't matter to him one way or another; this strong-minded man was going to do what he pleased. "Of course not," she assured him finally. "I'm delighted. I hate to eat alone."

He searched her face. Then, apparently satisfied, he nodded. Helping her off with her coat, he draped it over his arm with his jacket and Jill's pink parka. With his other arm he reached down to pick up Jill, who was grinning like an engaging elf. She held on tight to her father's neck as the three of them followed the woman past banks of potted poinsettias to a booth in the rear of the restaurant. Christmas carols played softly in the background.

"Would you like for me to take those?" the hostess asked, indicating the armload of coats.

"Yes, please," Holt answered. "And we'll need a booster chair."

"Certainly," said the woman, and disappeared through a swinging door.

"Can I sit by you, Libby?" Jill did a little dance when Holt stood her on the padded vinyl seat. She looked adorable in a yellow smocked dress that just covered her little bottom. Yellow tights protected her legs, and patent shoes were buckled across her insteps.

If the tights were slightly twisted, if the gold bar-rettes were askew among Jill's golden curls, it didn't matter, but Libby grinned inwardly at the picture of Holt struggling to dress the squirmy little body. She slid into the seat next to the child. "Of course, we'll sit to-gether," she told Jill. "I want to hear all about what you saw after we left the coffee shop."

Jill frowned in concentration. "I saw trucks and cars, lots of cars, and farmers," she said.

"Farms," Holt corrected as he sat opposite them. He had changed from the jeans of that morning into dark slacks and a sports coat. The blue dress shirt was a shade lighter than his eyes. "And tomorrow what will you see?" he prompted the child with an easy smile.

"Mountains—this big." Jill stood on her toes and stretched her hand high over her head. Her eyes rounded in wonder.

"That big, huh?"

"Bigger," pronounced the child with a sober nod.

Libby laughed. Her gaze returned to the man oppo-site. "She seems much more comfortable with you."

His smile tilted with a wry trace of embarrassment. "I had to resort to a bit of bribery to improve her mood, I'm afraid."

"And I saw four hotels," inserted Jill, tucking her thumb into a fist and examining her fingers before carefully spreading them out. "Four," she added with satisfaction.

"Four?" Libby's chuckle was directed toward Holt. "Couldn't you find one you liked?" she teased.

"It took us that long to find the one with your car in the lot. That was my bribe."

Libby remembered Jill's little woebegone face peering out from the back of the van as they left the truck stop, how quickly the tears had turned to smiles, and how easily Holt and Jill had parted from her the second time. She'd had her suspicions, but she wanted to hear him admit to the scheme. "You mean you were following me?" she asked in pretended surprise.

"Off and on until we got to Louisville. Right after we crossed the river we lost you in the traffic. You'll never know the panic I felt then. I don't think she would have forgiven me if I hadn't located your car."

He must be a pro. She hadn't even been aware of the van. Now that her suspicions were confirmed, she was surprised that she wasn't as uncomfortable with the idea as she would have expected to be.

The hostess reappeared with a booster chair. Libby hid her reaction under the fuss of getting Jill settled. No point in letting him know she was flattered.

"Thank you," Holt told the woman, who handed them the large parchment menus and placed a printed paper place mat in front of Jill.

"Enjoy your dinner," she said pleasantly, and left them alone.

Following her—that was why he had been so conveniently on the spot when she had slowed for the hitchhikers. He had made a promise to his daughter. He would go to a lot of trouble to avoid breaking such a promise. So much for flattery. She should have stuck to her original feelings of resentment at his interference.

Libby could imagine her family's reaction if they knew she was having dinner with a man she'd met this morning at a truck stop on the interstate. Her brothers would be through the roof, her sisters would be looking shocked and her mother would have fainted by now.

"Well," she said, opening the menu, "I guess it's a good thing you found me. You wouldn't have wanted to disappoint Jill."

Holt stayed her hand on the menu, caught her gaze and held it. When he spoke his voice was low and full of meaning. "I wouldn't have forgiven myself, either. I wanted to see you again, even more than my daughter did. We didn't part on the best of terms."

His slow smile was so warmly attractive, so engaging. Libby couldn't remember ever having met a man with such charisma. She was in danger of losing herself in the depths of his eyes.

He seemed to be waiting for an answer, or a comment, but she wasn't about to give one. And she wouldn't apologize for wanting to help the young man with the pregnant wife. With a small noncommittal smile, she willed her eyes away from his. "Are you hungry, Jill?" she asked brightly. "Look, you have your own menu with pictures. What do you think you'd like to eat?"

Jill studied the gaily printed paper in front of her. "That," she declared, pointing to the picture of a scrumptious ice-cream sundae.

"Naturally," said Libby, relaxing as she met Holt's grin. "That's for dessert, sweetheart. Dessert comes after dinner."

Jill gave a sly smile and tried again. "That," she said, watching her father for a reaction. It was a slice of pie à la mode. Holt shook his head and mouthed no.

Jill's lower lip came out in a resolute pout that was very adult.

Libby smothered her laughter and decided to try once more. "I think I'll have chicken," she told Jill. "Do you like chicken?"

"Okay," Jill answered in a resigned voice. "Then can we have dessert?"

"If your daddy says it's all right."

Jill turned those extraordinary eyes on her, but their expression was puzzled. "Do you have to ask him what you can eat, too?"

Holt met her amused expression with a chuckle. "It isn't easy to stay ahead of her, is it?"

"It's a struggle just to keep up, much less stay ahead of a child this age," Libby noted wryly. "She's about three, isn't she?"

Jill interrupted. "I'm almost four years old," she informed Libby, holding up four fingers again to prove her point.

"In January," added her father.

"You have your work cut out for you, Holt."

"I wouldn't have it any other way."

They finished dinner and lingered over some coffee as the restaurant slowly emptied. Conversation between them was casual, almost as though they were friends of long standing rather than new acquaintances. Comfortable, and surprised at the ease with which they talked, Libby found herself revealing a surprising amount of information, all the while wondering why. She usually opened up only to people she knew very well. The presence of the child, perhaps, accounted for her responsiveness, or maybe the man's easygoing temperament was responsible.

She learned a lot about him, too—that he was thirty-four, that he was a cattle rancher and also had citrus groves not far from TOLTOT.

"I started out with cattle and expanded into fruit about ten years ago when a grove adjoining my property came up for sale. I had begun to cut back on my herds, but I'm relieved I didn't get out of the cattle business altogether." Holt stirred his coffee and set the spoon in the saucer. "The citrus industry has been through some really bad times for the past three years, what with the weather and the citrus canker that swept the nurseries in the central part of the state last year."

"I remember reading about that in the newspaper, and watching the news and seeing the trees being burned. What is the canker exactly?" She propped her chin on her knuckles.

"It's a small spore that spreads like measles. The spore doesn't hurt the fruit, but it can kill a tree in one year, and it takes many years for a tree to grow to its full potential for harvest. I was lucky, I escaped. But a lot of the growers have lost everything." He picked up his cup to take a sip. "That's enough talk about depressing topics. Tell me more about Libby Hamilton. I already know you come from a large family."

Libby leaned back in the booth. Resting her head against the cushions, she smiled at the question and her lack of hesitation in answering. "My parents have been married for thirty-eight years, and I'm the youngest of five children. I've worked for a computer firm in Chicago ever since I graduated from college. I have—had—my own apartment and earned a good salary. Yet they still treated me as if I was sixteen years old. This move to Florida is my belated bid for independence."

"How old are you?" Holt asked.

"Twenty-seven."

"You look younger," he commented.

She sighed. "I always have, unfortunately. My timing for this move wasn't the best. My folks were horrified that I wouldn't be home for Christmas. They're wonderful people. But they can't let go. As a result we are slightly estranged at the moment."

Jill had long since disposed of the booster chair and was fast asleep on the seat, her head in Libby's lap. Libby idly played with the child's golden curls, twirling one around her finger, where it clung lovingly. "What about your family?"

"The only family I have are assorted cousins scattered all over the country. I was an only child, and both my parents are dead. I live alone—or did until now—in a house that's much too big, but it was built by my great-grandfather." He shrugged. "I suppose I'm a sentimentalist to hold on to it."

Libby tried to hide her smile, but it was nice to hear a man admit to such a thing. "There's nothing wrong with being a sentimentalist. It's a good trait in a father. I imagine Jill will make quite a difference in your life."

Holt grinned ruefully. "It will be an adjustment. But I've been anxious to have Jill with me."

"Did you...?" Libby bit her lip to hold back the question. The circumstances surrounding the custody of his daughter were none of her business. She sipped quickly from her cup.

Holt answered her unspoken question. "My former wife is an actress. She's planning a move to New York that we agreed would not be the best thing for Jill. While she lived in Chicago, the nurse who raised my wife lived with them. Nana was a wonderful, loving woman, and I didn't worry too much about Jill as long as she was around. But she had grown too old to cope, especially with a move to New York, so she's retired now."

"Then you didn't have a disagreement over custody?"

"Oh, yes. We had that, but we didn't have to resort to a court battle to solve it. Linda was quite reasonable." His mouth twisted. "Her career has always been her priority."

Was he still in love with his ex-wife, wondered Libby, concealing her speculative look beneath her thick lashes. And why was the possibility disturbing? She answered her own question honestly. Because even though their acquaintance was brief, this man affected her more acutely, more completely than any other man had ever done. Now was not the time to become involved. But, she rationalized, it would be nice to know someone in the town where she was going to make her home.

The waiter came by with a pot of coffee. "May I give you folks another refill?"

Libby's hand hovered above her cup. She declined with a smile. "None for me, thank you."

Holt shook his head and the waiter moved on.

She looked around to find they were the last customers. "I think I'd better call it a day," she said. "I didn't realize the drive would tire me so much." Jill moved restlessly when Libby sat up straight against the padded booth. She smiled down at the sleeping child. "If you lift her carefully, she probably won't even wake up."

Holt met her smile with a frown. He seemed to be trying to make up his mind about something. Finally he reached out to cover her hand with one of his. "Look, Libby. Since we're traveling in the same direction, why don't we drive together?"

Libby caught her breath at the surge of heat that traveled swiftly up her arm at the touch. Her voice seemed to be stuck somewhere in her throat. Her electric response to him reinforced her idea that he was dangerous to her peace of mind. Even earlier, when he'd used those fantastic eyes to mesmerize her, she'd been able to guard against revealing too much of the effect he had on her. But he hadn't touched her then. All it took was one touch for the tremors of awareness to begin again, for the sensual perception to spring back to life, leaving her shaken under the force of his masculinity.

Holt had loosened the top buttons of the blue shirt, lending the atmosphere between them an offhand sort of hominess that in the blink of an eye became intimate.

"I promise not to make a pest of myself," he went on in a low voice, his thumb massaging the back of her hand. "But a beautiful woman, traveling alone... I'd feel better about you, if you'd let me stay close. Especially after what happened this afternoon."

Inadvertently he had broken the spell by assuming she would readily agree. Libby sat up, her spine ramrod straight, and withdrew her hand. The comment was just the impetus she needed to pull herself together. Perversely, she probably would have consented if he'd said he wanted to get to know her better. Instead he had to bring up the hitchhikers. She didn't need anyone to shield her from the big bad world.

Holt was an appealing magnetic man, but she was uprooting her life to escape just this kind of autocratic interest in her well-being. Now here she was, less than one day out of Chicago, and someone else was willing to make her decisions, to look after her. At that moment she resolved to have nothing further to do with Holt Whitney. Saddened by the decision, she nevertheless knew it was necessary.

"Thanks for your concern, but I'm not sure what my schedule will be. And I'm sorry for the delay in your trip when you went back to help those poor people. You should have let me go."

"You know I didn't mean that," Holt grated under his breath. "I didn't mind helping them. I just didn't want you doing it."

"That attitude is very annoying, you know."

"Sorry," he answered, not sounding sorry at all.

Jill whimpered and stirred in unconscious reaction to their irritated words. Her sleepy eyes opened to look up from Libby's lap. Then she scrambled to her feet on the seat and glanced around as though she wasn't sure where she was. She popped her thumb into her mouth.

"It's all right, baby." Libby automatically held out her arms. After only a second's hesitation the small warm body cuddled into them quite naturally. "She should be in bed," Libby told Holt, grateful the conversation had been suspended.

"I know," he said. He reached for the check, but Libby was quicker.

"My treat," she said with far too much good humor in her voice to be convincing. "You bought my gasoline this morning." The truth was, she refused to be any more beholden to this man than she already was.

Holt started to argue, but one look at her stubborn chin and he relented. "Only if I can take care of breakfast." He pulled some bills out of his pocket and left them on the table for a tip.

Libby wavered. This situation was becoming ridiculous. He might as well adopt her. Rather than argue, she agreed readily. "All right." She had already made up her mind. She needed to put this incident behind her and get on with the trip. There had been a notice in her room that the coffee shop opened at six. Tomorrow morning she would be long gone before Holt and Jill were even awake.

Holt bent to take his daughter from Libby's arms. Libby rose and followed them across the restaurant. While she took care of the check, he helped a sleepy Jill into her coat and arranged the hood over her blond curls. The child fussed irritably, pushing the hood away. "No," she complained.

Holt pulled it back into place. "Poor baby, you're sleepy," he crooned. "But you don't want your ears to get cold, do you?"

"Yes," answered Jill contrarily.

The child didn't demur, however, when Libby took over the task. "There, all buttoned up against the cold. And you'll be in your bed in just a few minutes."

"Will you tuck me in my bed, Libby?" she asked, watching with wide eyes as Libby slid her arms into her own coat. "Please?" The child turned to her father without waiting for an answer. "I want Libby to tuck me in." She looked up at him as though doubting his ability to deliver what she wanted, while at the same time holding her arms up for him to lift her. "I asked nice," she added when she was balanced on his hip.

"Do you mind?" he asked Libby, his eyes dark with amusement, knowing she couldn't refuse.

"No, of course not," Libby answered, resigned...for now.

Holt took her arm with his free hand. "Let's go, then."

The Whitneys' room was on the second floor, above and several doors away from hers. Holt shifted Jill to his other hip and delved into the pocket of his slacks to come up with a key, which he fitted into the lock. A burst of hot air hit them in the face. "Oh, Lord. Jill, have you been playing with the thermostat?"

"Hmm," said the child in feigned innocence. She wiggled to be free, and he let her slide down his leg to the floor. "Come in, Libby," she said politely.

Leaving the door ajar, Holt crossed to the heater that was in a unit under the windows. Jill followed her father and watched him bend down to peer into the mechanism. He turned his head until he was nose to nose with his daughter. "High?" he asked calmly.

"I was cold," she defended herself sincerely. "You turned the car on high when I was cold."

"But you can't read." He shook his head, stupefied by her seeming ability to reason.

Jill shrugged. "It looked the same. I'll get my pajamas." She had unfastened her coat and dropped it on the floor. Reaching into an open suitcase on one of the beds, she rummaged around for a minute, strewing clothes on the bed, the floor before finally coming up with a pair of fuzzy-looking pajamas. She climbed onto the bed and stood in the middle of the mattress. "Will you unbutton my dress?" she asked Libby.

"Certainly." Libby complied, barely able to hold her laughter in check. Holt was in for one surprise after another if he thought children weren't smarter than he expected them to be. Before she removed the child's dress, she suggested that Holt close the door. "It didn't take long for the room to cool off, did it?" she said, chatting as she helped Jill into the pajamas. "There now, are you ready for bed?"

"I still have to brush my teeth," Jill said to her, as though Libby should have known. Stomach first, she slid off the mattress and disappeared into the bathroom.

Libby looked at Holt and burst out laughing. She caught the arm of a chair and sank down. "Don't worry. You'll get used to it. I have a nephew the same age."

"But she can't read," repeated the perplexed man. He stood with his feet planted apart, hands jammed into his pockets.

"No, but they seem to see a picture of the word. They don't know what it means, only that it will do what they want. Have you ever seen one who didn't know what the 'on' button on a television was for?"

"I thought I was so smart, consulting a psychologist," he mused, taking a place on the edge of the bed, facing Libby. He leaned forward, his elbows on his knees, his fingers linked together loosely. "She doesn't have any children, come to think of it."

"It won't take long to get used to the antics of a three-year-old."

"Almost four," he reminded her with a grin. "She's really a smart little devil, isn't she?"

"Brilliant," agreed Libby, biting her lip.

"I guess all parents think their children are the smartest. At least she's showing some signs of spirit." His expression saddened. "I was worried when I picked her up, because she was so quiet. With the exception of her stubbornness over the rest room this morning, she's obeyed me blindly, responding like a little automaton. She never argued and looked at me as if I was a stranger from another planet."

"Well, you're obviously doing all the right things, because she's much more relaxed with you than she was then."

"She's really taken to you, too. I think that's helped."

Libby was immediately on guard again. "Yes, well, I told you, I've had a lot of experience."

Before she realized his intention, Holt reached for her hand and held it firmly between his own. Short of struggling against his determination, she couldn't free herself, so she relaxed.

"Libby, why are you so defensive?" His voice was an octave lower than it had been. He seemed to ask the question out of curiosity.

Libby sighed. "I told you. This move is my bid for independence. I do like your daughter, Holt."

"And her father?"

He looked so appealing that she had to smile. "Yes, her father, too. But I don't want to get involved."

"You didn't feel like that until I mentioned traveling together."

She wasn't really surprised at his perceptiveness. "You're right." After thinking for a minute she decided to be completely honest. "I'm afraid it's a conditioned reflex whenever someone tries to take charge of me. My family wanted to be in on every facet of my life, from my decorating to my dates. More than anything right now, I need some privacy to be my own person."

"Your family must love you very much," Holt observed quietly.

A note of wistfulness had roughened his voice. Libby searched his expression, but nothing there reflected his change of mood. She must have imagined it. "And I love them," she answered. "I'm going to miss them a lot, but I want to be myself for a change. Can you understand that?"

"I'm not sure. I've always thought it would be nice to have a big family, but maybe it's rough on the youngest."

Libby hesitated. "I'm not a militant feminist still, men have a definite advantage when it comes to independence. My parents would never have dreamed of interfering in my brothers' lives. And you wouldn't have minded if a man had wanted to pick up a hitchhiker. Would you? You would just have thought it was his own business and driven on."

"I'm ready," a small voice piped up from the bathroom door. Holt was grateful for the interruption, giving him a breathing space to absorb the rather personal turn the conversation had taken.

When Jill had been tucked in and kissed and hugged, her eyes drooping sleepily, he was still trying to decide how to answer Libby's question without sounding like a first-rate chauvinist.

He couldn't tell her, for instance, that she inspired chivalrous, protective impulses. He turned out the wall lamp between the beds and stood looking down at his daughter for a long minute.

Libby returned to the chair she'd occupied before, in the only circle of light left in the room. Finally he came back to sit on the bed facing her. "Libby, you're a very feminine, and as I told you, a very desirable woman," he began.

She interrupted, keeping her voice low so as not to disturb the child. "You've known me for less than twelve hours, and already you're trying to make my decisions for me. Just for curiosity's sake, why does this protectiveness come out? I'm twenty-seven years old, I have a good job." She surged to her feet, halting in front of him, her hands knotting into fists at her sides. "I don't understand it at all, and I like it even less. Why do people seem to have this urge to look out for me?"

"Hey," he cautioned, glancing across at Jill, who was sleeping soundly now. "You're overreacting."

The accusation irritated her. Her eyes sparkled pewter. "Am I? I don't think so. I seem to bring out the autocrat in the nicest men."

"Hold it! A friendly offer to travel together doesn't make me an autocrat. Did you ever stop to think that I was simply concerned about you as a woman traveling alone? Part of the reason is your nature. It's immediately apparent to any stranger that you're a very warm and giving person."

She shot him a disbelieving look, and he went on. "It's true. Look at the way you rushed in to help Jill, and you would have picked up the hitchhikers even though you knew you shouldn't."

"Those were exceptions. As a rule I never talk to strangers."

He moved his shoulders in a dismissive shrug that annoyed her even more. "You talked to me easily enough."

She couldn't deny that. "You said that's part of it. What's the rest?" she demanded.

Holt wasn't sure when the conversation had deteriorated to a wrangle but he didn't particularly mind. She stood over him like an accusing angel. He resisted the very real urge to yank her down on the bed beside him, kiss her breathless and make her forget this argument. Instead he slapped his knees and got to his feet. "Look, Libby..." He shook his head, trying to find the right words, and she took the gesture for a negative.

"Please, Holt," she urged, her anger forgotten.

Uncontrollably, his hands shot out to grasp her shoulders lightly. "I'll give the truth to you, then," he said, his eyes roaming her face. Her skin was almost translucent. "My reaction, at least, and I guarantee it has nothing to do with wanting to protect you, golden girl."

He took a long breath. "I imagine you know how you look, because you see yourself in the mirror every morning, but I'll explain my particular response. You are the picture of femininity, as graceful as a gazelle when you move, long delicate fingers, a waist so tiny it's a tormenting temptation to a man to see if he can span it with his hands."

His fingers crept across her shoulder to the side of her neck. They tangled in her hair and came to rest just beneath her ear over the pulse there, which had begun to race wildly. Her skin felt silky, slightly damp under the weight of her hair, and she smelled of tropical flowers.

"Your hair is the color of summer sunshine, warm and lustrous," he continued. "There is a trace of a blue vein in your temple that is fascinating, and your mouth—" he shuddered "—oh Lord, your mouth is tempting. Even wearing that bulky sweater you had on this morning, I knew you had beautiful breasts, a lovely shape. In other words, lady, you are an incredibly sexy creature."

Her smoky eyes looked stunned, and she was silent. He hadn't meant to upset her. He drew her forward until their lips were only a breath apart. "Protection is the last thing on my mind, Libby. You should be protecting yourself from me, because from the moment I saw you I've wanted to make love to you." His lips played at the corner of hers, giving her time to pull away.

Libby blinked rapidly, knowing she should protest, but she couldn't seem to find the will or the strength. Each of her senses was achingly, intensely alive. Her hands stirred restlessly against his chest, unsure whether to push or caress.

"You can slap my face if you want, but you did ask," he whispered, leaving little kisses across her lips. His breath was warm and sweet.

As Holt watched through slitted eyes, Libby's long lashes fell in submission. His name escaped her lips on a soft sigh and, at last, she relaxed against him, sending a surge of desire through his blood like liquid fire.

He moved slowly, spreading his fingers, sliding his hand around to her back and carefully fitting her to his length. Despite the contrast in size, it took very little adjustment for their bodies to come into perfect alignment. She felt so damn good. He covered her mouth briefly, withdrew, shifted the angle and touched her full lower lip with his tongue.

Immediately he felt her open to him. He couldn't control the muted groan that escaped or the sudden constriction of his arm at her back. Her breasts were crushed to his chest, burning against him, as he deepened the kiss. The honeyed, miraculous taste of her tongue as it met his sent his senses spinning, his heart galloping in rhythm to the pulse under his fingers. The hand at her neck slid up into her hair, holding her head immovable.

He hadn't reacted to a woman in this way, since he was twenty. And this was neither the time nor the place for his arousal to be appeased. Jill might awaken, or he might turn this beautiful woman off for good. But,

Lord, just one more minute, just one more taste. His hands ached to touch her breasts.

A whimper from her throat, felt in his, brought him back to reality. At the sound, he lifted his head. His breathing was harsh, but he managed to whisper soothing, if broken phrases into her hair. "It's all right. I didn't mean. . .to move so fast, honey. Okay? Libby. . .?"

"Holt. . .this isn't. . .I can't. . ." Libby took advantage of his slackening embrace to pull free. Her pulse was as unsteady as her voice, and the blood coursing through her veins was hot and thick. It wasn't resistance that had prompted the whimper, but pure, unadulterated desire, sexual hunger and a basic need for fulfillment that she hadn't felt in a long, long time. She had fallen into the arms of this man as though she had always belonged there.

She dropped her head forward to hide her expression. "I have to go," she whispered.

"I'll walk you to your room."

Her blond head came back up. "No. Jill might wake up alone. She'd be scared." She looked around in a daze for her purse and coat. Picking them up from the floor, she concentrated on getting out of there. "I'm right downstairs and only a few doors away."

"Libby, I'm really sorry if I insulted you."

"You didn't," she assured him. "I scared the daylights out of myself, that's all. I don't usually. . . You're very potent."

Holt grinned widely, the blue eyes sparkling in amusement at her honesty. He had been correct in his first assessment of this woman. She was one in a million. "I'm glad."

She looked away, then back, knowing it was a mistake. His expression was tender and amused. She met the small smile with one of her own. "I'm not. I'm feeling rather exasperated with myself. Good night, Holt." She moved to the door.

"Good night, Libby. We'll see you at seven for breakfast," he said to her back as she descended the steel-railed concrete steps.

She didn't answer. He leaned out over the balcony to see that she made it safely to her room. Just before she closed the door, she turned to give a tired wave.

Holt reentered his room, shrugging out of his jacket. With a heavy sigh, he lay across the bed and hooked his hands behind his head. As he stared at the ceiling, his thoughts were filled with the woman who had just put a large hole in his self-proclaimed control. He wondered why he had reacted so strongly to her. When he had found out this morning that she was moving to his hometown, his intention had been to get her into bed; but now he found he wanted more. He wanted to know her…and he asked himself why.

He rubbed his eyes with thumb and forefinger. And why had he suggested they travel together? He certainly didn't need any more responsibility. Not right now. Jill would put a definite dent in his life-style as it was. She was a dent he welcomed, but nonetheless, his life was going to be greatly altered.

Linda wasn't the villain in their divorce; circumstances were. They had married too young, in college, when the possibility of pregnancy had arisen. That had been a false alarm, but he hadn't cared. He had thought he loved her.

Through the ten years they were married, she grew more and more restless and irritable. And he grew more and more impatient and withdrawn. It was a marriage that never should have been. Linda tried in her own way to make it work, but the draw of the stage was too strong. Holt bore her no ill will. In fact, he liked her much better now that they were no longer man and wife.

Jill was the result of a mistaken idea on Linda's part that a child might complete her life, stifle the stage-struck urges. Shortly after she was born they both realized that having the child, though they both loved her, hadn't saved the marriage. As they broke one vow, they made another—Jill would never be the one to suffer for their failure.

Once he recovered from the feelings of betrayal associated with divorce, he became accustomed to the single life, even began to enjoy the freedom from responsibility that he'd never had in his adult life. If he occasionally felt bored with shallow relationships, he told himself that was better than being tied down.

Women were attracted to successful men, ready to offer the consolation they were sure was needed, and he reveled in their willingness. He made certain they understood that he wasn't interested in permanency. He learned to avoid the trap of commitment, a trap he swore to himself he'd never walk into again. And he learned to say goodbye, easily, without a backward glance.

Libby Hamilton was a beautiful woman, but so were several others he was acquainted with. This chance encounter shouldn't change anything, yet for some reason it did. He wasn't sure what made her different. He tried once again to put her into a familiar slot, a classification; she refused to stay there.

When Linda had made up her mind to try for success in New York, he'd gained custody of Jill with the least amount of fuss. Now he had his family. Jill was all he needed. Not a woman. Not now, not for a long time. Perhaps not ever.

THE SPITTING SNOW of the morning had turned to a full-fledged storm by early afternoon. She couldn't be too far from Nashville, thought Libby. The waiter at the motel where she'd stopped for breakfast—carefully parking her car behind the building—had told her she would have a three- to four-hour drive, depending on weather conditions. Even allowing for the snow, which had slowed her speed considerably, and the mountainous terrain, she should have been there by now.

Afraid to take her eyes off the road long enough to glance at the clock, she remained hunched over the wheel. Her shoulders ached with tension, her eyes were glued to the faint suggestion of a center line. If she dared glance away, the blurred guide might disappear. It seemed as though she'd been driving through the white swirling mist of a netherworld forever. A gust of wind, stronger than any before, swept a colorless curtain, more dense than before, across her view and threatened to wrest control of the car from her hands. She gripped the wheel tighter. Damn her pride. Why hadn't she agreed to travel with Holt?

Her mind's eye easily conjured up a picture of him, large and rugged and infinitely appealing, and she could hear the echo of his husky chuckle. The gaudy van was large and heavy. He wouldn't have trouble keeping his vehicle on the road. Or maybe he was really smart and wasn't on the road at all, but snug in some restaurant having lunch. On cue, her stomach growled.

Instead she had sneaked out of the motel before seven and driven away like a truant so they wouldn't meet. Now she was in a messy, if not downright dangerous situation. Surely there would be a motel soon, and surely the weather would clear enough for her to see it. At the last exit she had steered onto the exit ramp, only to find herself at the intersection of…nowhere, with no motel, no service station, no restaurant, only a tired sign saying that accommodations were seventeen miles to the east.

She had decided at that point that the major highway was safer to travel on. The traffic had become almost nonexistent then. She hadn't seen another vehicle in the past ten miles at least. Nor could she pick up anything on the radio. The silence was as thick as a blanket, except for the harsh sound of her breathing and the muffled hum of the engine. She might be the last person on the face of the earth.

Was it her imagination, or were the wipers slowing down? The color of the hood was completely obliterated by snow, which was piling up against the edge of the windshield. As she watched in horror, they slowed even more under the weight of frozen snow.

For the first time Libby really tasted fear, metallic and bitter at the back of her throat, spilling into her nostrils, burning her eyes. Until now she had acknowledged that this was a horrifying experience, but not that she could die. Suddenly dying was a very real possibility. *Oh, God! What will my family say?* "I told you so," she answered her own question. *Yes, Mom, Dad...you told me so.*

Holt...what would have happened if she hadn't been so quick to deny, so impatient to run from the attraction between them? She would be sitting in that restaurant with him, sipping hot coffee and discussing the weather. And Jill would be curled up on the seat beside her, while his fantastic blue eyes told her things he couldn't say aloud in front of the child.

Libby choked back a sob that verged on hysteria and blinked rapidly to keep her eyes clear. *Don't cry, for heaven's sake,* she admonished herself sternly. *Crying won't help one bit. The thing to do is to keep your wits about you and think of a way out of this.*

But Mother Nature seemed to have the upper hand. The wipers ground to a halt with a protesting squeal.

Jamming on the brakes, Libby felt the car swerve slightly, but mercifully it halted with all four tires still on the pavement. Afraid to pull off to the shoulder in case she never found the road again, she thrust the gearshift into park, pulled out the hazard switch to activate the blinking lights and opened the door before she could change her mind. She put her head out into a white hell where she could neither see nor breathe. She leaned across the hinge of the door to scrub at the windshield with her bare hand.

The bitter cold took immediate advantage, invading the woolen fabric of her sweater and slacks as easily as though penetrating chiffon, licking greedily at her skin. Using touch rather than sight, she clawed frantically at the build-up of snow around the base of the wipers.

One finger caught on a rough piece of metal, but the cold was so numbing that she didn't even know she'd been cut. The curtain of snow seemed to fill space more densely than air, suffocating her lungs with frozen crystals.

Finally the wiper shuddered and moved under her hand, then picked up its sluggish rhythm.

Libby grinned. "Bless your mechanical little heart!" she shouted over the wind and eased back inside the car. Slamming the door, she breathed gratefully and shook the snow out of her hair with a toss of her head. Rubbing her hands together in an attempt to restore the circulation, she suddenly felt encouraged. *You're going to make it, Libby. You're really going to make it!* She swiped a shaking hand down her face, oblivious to the streak of blood left there, and determinedly put the gearshift in drive. It was then that she realized the car was stuck. She alternated between drive and reverse in an attempt to rock it free.

Drive, then reverse. But the car refused to move. She increased the pressure on the accelerator, only to groan aloud as the tires spun uselessly.

"No!" she cried, beating at the wheel with an impotent fist. "A piece of machinery is *not* going to do this to me!" In furious desperation, she slammed her foot all the way to the floor.

The car leaped forward, out of control on the icy asphalt. It gyrated, the wheel spinning free through Libby's palms, and the violent swerve jerked her head sideways to crack against the window. Finally the vehicle came to rest, nose down in a ditch. She made a valiant effort to remain conscious, but the struggle was futile and, at last, as she moaned softly, her head fell back to the headrest, and she closed her eyes over helpless tears.

But hope dies hard, and Holt Whitney was her only hope. He alone in the whole world knew, even approximately, where she was.

All was silent. Mother Nature had her revenge against machine and man. Her retribution would have been complete...except for the silent burst of the rear hazard signal, flashing steadily through the swirling snow, the fading light of afternoon, as constant and dependable as the wink of a computer's cursor.

GOD, HELP ME FIND HER...Dear God, please...please! Heading north, Holt had passed three exits and doubled back toward the south. The little fool, he ranted mentally for the hundredth time.

Libby hadn't gotten away as easily as she'd thought this morning. Holt and Jill were leaving their room when he caught sight of her car pulling out of the parking lot. He had thought about going after her, then dismissed the idea. Let her go. Repeating the reflections of last night, he told himself that he didn't need the complication of a woman in his life right now. He could call her, later, in a month or so, when she had gotten used to her new job.

The storm had taken the weather forecasters by surprise. When the driving conditions had worsened an hour ago, he had tried to tell himself Libby wouldn't take chances in weather like this. But somehow, from somewhere, came a feeling of unease that couldn't be silenced by calm rationalization. Something was very wrong, and he felt it gut-deep, with a chilling force that quickly grew to panic. Something was very wrong.

Gripping the steering wheel, he blessed the chance that had caused him to buy the vehicle in Chicago, where snow tires were standard equipment, rather than Florida. Even with the heavy-duty tires and even considering the weight of the van, he was having trouble keeping to a straight line against the intense power of the wind.

He had almost passed the point where Libby was stranded—when an intermittent flash caught his eye. He stopped breathing. Carefully he toed the brake, using coercion to slow the van until it came to a complete stop. He was out of the vehicle, striding back along the road toward the blinking light, praying softly, "God, please...just one more miracle...just one more..."

The windows were iced over, the door latch frozen shut, but with a superhuman wrench he had it open. The car was empty. Holt was stunned for a moment, then hopeless fury welled up with the bile in his throat. "Damn you," he whispered. His words were captured effortlessly, muffled by the force of the wind.

Stop. Stop and think. This was no time to descend to emotionalism. There was still a chance...a slim, almost nonexistent chance...and as long— Furious at the moisture that threatened to blind him, he brought his gloved hand down with a powerful slam on the top of the car.

"Holt!"

He was dreaming.

"Holt!"

The snow-covered figure rose from behind the front fender on the opposite side of the car and stumbled toward him. A snow shovel dangled from one hand. Before he could take more than a step, she dropped the shovel, careering into his outstretched arms. They closed around her like a vise.

He put his cheek to her precious face. Her skin was like ice.

"Libby, oh God, Libby. . ." he choked. His eyes squeezed shut. When they opened, a flare seemed to light the blue depths as he slid his arms around her shoulders and under her legs, lifting her in his arms. In bare seconds he covered the ground between the two vehicles and had her inside the heated van.

Holt placed her on the padded bench seat in the back and ripped off his coat, wrapping her in its folds, warm from his body heat. Then he pulled her back into his arms, burying his face in her neck. Her slight body shivered against him, and he began to kiss her eyes, her lips, her cheeks, her forehead, letting his breath warm her skin. "Libby. . .Libby. . .Libby." Her name was a litany of thanksgiving on his lips as they roamed over her face.

Libby was dreaming. Cold as eternity on the outside, she felt a warmth building around her heart, spreading with each beat like golden honey through her veins, offsetting the chills that racked her body. Holt was kissing her, holding her; this had to be a dream. She was almost afraid to open her eyes for fear the dream might disappear, but at last she lifted her lashes, surprised at how heavy they were. "Holt," she murmured. Her lips and tongue felt numb as she formed the word. "Thank you. I was so scared. I was trying to scrape the snow from under the wheels, but it kept blowing back." She choked on a laugh. "Thank you."

His head jerked up. The feeling she saw burning from his eyes brought tears to her own. "Oh, Holt," she said with a sob. "It's like a miracle." Her fingers clenched into fists in the fabric of his shirt.

He held her with one arm while the other hand came up to brush back her hair. "You have a bruise here," he said, the touch of his fingers at her temple as light as a butterfly's kiss. "And blood. But I don't see a cut anywhere."

"I bumped my head when I went into the ditch. It's okay. I really appreciate your coming back for me."

His hand trembled slightly. "Don't you know that I couldn't have done anything else?" He spread his fingers over her cheeks, and his thumb caressed her chin. "Oh, honey, don't you know...?" he whispered just before his mouth came down on hers.

The kiss held no hint of sensuality. It was a deeply caring kiss, one of relief and tenderness and gratitude. He held her close in a powerful and protective embrace that she didn't mind at all.

When it ended, Holt continued to hold her, rocking her slightly, staring over her head at an illusive vision. The woman in his arms breathed and moved. The overwhelming fear he had felt at the thought that she could have been at this very moment cold and lifeless sent a wave of protectiveness through him that he knew she wouldn't appreciate, and he shouldn't be feeling.

Emotion, part self-protection, part exasperation, part relief, took shape in anger. Keeping her tight against him, he shook her weakly. "You fool. I could wring your neck. Why didn't you wait this morning?"

Libby had lived all her life with two brothers and a father who reacted to danger with angry words. "Just dumb, I guess," she answered quietly.

Sure enough, she didn't have to defend herself; he justified her actions for her. "I guess I came on too strong for you."

They stayed like that, holding each other for a long time, the only sound the purr of the engine and the brave whine of the van's heater. Finally Libby stirred against Holt's restraining hold, and he immediately loosened his arms. Their eyes met. They smiled, both a little self-conscious at the intensity of the emotion they'd shared. Finally she tore her eyes away from his and looked around. "Where's Jill?"

Holt smiled down at her. "You won't believe where she is. I left her with a farm couple down the road, total strangers." He shook his head as though he couldn't believe it himself.

"What? Where? How could you...?"

"Easy, honey. There is a camaraderie among farmers, a sort of built-in inclination to help each other out. I had to come after you. It was...I don't know...an impression that you needed me. A very strong impression. I couldn't ignore it, but I couldn't bring her into a dangerous situation, either. So I looked for the nearest farmhouse with bicycles on the front porch."

Libby struggled to sit up. "We have to go back for her, Holt. Now. She must be scared to death."

"I know," he answered, releasing her reluctantly. "I should get you to a doctor, too. That bump on your head could be serious."

"I don't need a doctor for a little bump on the head. I barely have a headache." Which was a lie; her head was throbbing. "A couple of aspirins, and I'll be fine."

Holt looked at her dubiously but he didn't argue. "I'll get your things from your car." He picked up his jacket from where he'd flung it over her feet and shrugged into it.

"Thanks." She caught his hand. The thanks was for more than the offer to get her things, and he knew it. He leaned down to cover her lips in another hard kiss.

As soon as their lips met, the heat flamed to a conflagration, out of control. Libby wound her arms tightly around his neck, moving against him in an instinctive effort to be closer.

Neither was prepared for the explosion. They drew apart to drag in unsteady breaths. Then, closing his eyes, Holt blindly felt for her mouth again, parting her teeth with a thrusting tongue. Her lips were warm now, and silky, and they brought him to a sudden unexpected arousal. Wild, crazy desire slammed through him.

It was a celebration of life, a grateful celebration that stirred their senses so completely that he would have made love with her there on the floor of the van, in the middle of a raging snowstorm, if she hadn't made a sound deep in her throat, recalling them to the present. He wrenched his mouth away to bury his face in the cloud of sunshine that was her hair. "You want to know something crazy? I want you. Now."

Libby gave a halting little laugh, as he released her. "I know," she answered breathlessly. "But I guess it would be smarter to get out of here."

He cradled her face in his broad hands and smiled. "Definitely smarter."

"Yes, we'd better get going," she agreed shakily.

When Holt slid back the loading door of the van, Libby was surprised to see that the storm was still raging full force. Inside, in the warmth of his arms, it was almost possible to forget why they were there in the first place, because of her stubbornness. It was her fault that he'd left his daughter in the care of strangers, so that he could come back for her in the middle of a storm. She sat up, her spine rigid.

He had said he'd felt something...the same mental link she'd experienced just before she'd passed out, as though there was an extraordinary line of communication between them. This sort of thing had never happened to her before, not even with intimate family members. The sensation was eerie, but she didn't question the fact that the bond between them had saved her life.

Holt was back in only a few minutes. His dark hair and brows were white. He heaved her two suitcases, coat and purse inside, and disappeared again.

"Holt, wait!" she called as he slammed the door. He could leave the rest. They needed to get out of there, and they needed to do it in a hurry.

"You didn't have to bring it all," she told him when he returned with her portable computer and the shopping bags full of Christmas presents from her family.

"Unless you wanted your car vandalized, I did," he said, tossing her the keys. "An unattended car is a temptation. Maybe you'll be lucky." Without further conversation, he climbed into the driver's seat and put the van in gear. "There's some coffee in the thermos under your seat," he offered with a smile when she moved up to sit beside him. "I imagine something hot would be good right now, wouldn't it?"

"Mmm, yes." She reached down. "Can I pour you some?"

"If you don't mind holding it for me. I'm going to need both hands on the wheel."

Silently she filled two cups and sipped at one. When he indicated he wanted a swallow, she held the cup carefully. The wind buffeted them mercilessly now that they were moving again, but the weight of the van gave it a secure steadiness on the road. She was surprised at how the vertical windshield stayed clearer of snow than her slanted one. Their vision was better, but at the same time their precarious situation was more evident. The snow, already banked by the side of the highway, had begun to creep across the pavement.

"It isn't much farther," said Holt, seeming to read her thoughts. He steered carefully onto an off ramp and slowed as the van tilted on the incline. When they reached the crossroad, he let out his breath and grinned quickly. "Next driveway to the right. Help me keep a lookout for the turn."

"Okay." Relief flooded through Libby at the knowledge that the nightmare was almost over. She released her grasp on the door, not realizing how tightly she'd been gripping it until her fingers began to tingle in response. "There! Is that the drive?"

"That's it," he affirmed with a laugh of triumph. "We made it!"

The warmth of lanterns splashed welcoming yellow paths across the snow from the windows of the Victorian house. Two stories tall, the building gave the impression of having stood there forever. Gingerbread rimmed the roof of the broad porch that crossed the front and sides of the first floor.

To Libby, the house was the most beautiful sight in the world. But along with her relief—the knowledge that they were safe—reaction set in. Fatigue settled over her like a blanket.

The boundaries of the drive were obliterated by the snowfall, but Holt drove without hesitation to a spot under a bare oak tree about thirty feet from the steps. The front door opened, spilling out more light.

"Libby, I told these people...well, I didn't exactly *tell* them...but I needed help."

"What?" Her headache was returning, not a blinding pain, but a dull throb. She was too tired to figure out why he seemed disconcerted.

"They might be under the impression that we're married," he said, opening the door of the van to hop down before she had a chance to comment on the startling remark. The snow swirled inside before he shut the door. He came around to help Libby out on her side, in effect putting the van between them and the house for a moment.

"Why would they have that impression?" she asked calmly as he reached for her.

"Need any help?" a female voice shouted.

"Thanks, I can manage!" Holt shouted back.

He swung her up into his arms. "What was I going to say? That I was leaving my child with strangers to go back for a gorgeous woman I met yesterday? Actually, I didn't have to say much at all. Jill told them she was moving to Florida, and the woman just assumed you were my wife and we had gotten separated in the storm. I was in too big a rush to straighten it out then."

"And what do you plan to tell her now? I suppose we'll have to stay here?" Libby asked quietly, realizing what a ridiculous question that was. The snow seemed to have slackened momentarily, but this storm was far from over.

Holt had to bend his head to hear her. At her words he gave her an unbelieving look, shaking his head. "What do you think? None of us is going out in this storm again."

"Of course not. It was stupid of me to ask."

He grinned down at her, and she felt that same weakness in her limbs. The snow was building up in his hair again, and she had to resist the urge to brush it away.

He circled the van, his head still close to hers. His voice was deep and intimate. "I don't suppose you'd go along with sharing a bedroom?" He lifted a brow and tried to suppress the chuckle that shook his body.

"You don't suppose right," she muttered under her breath, her hand going to her temple.

Holt's eyes narrowed when he saw the pain in hers. "You are hurting," he accused softly.

"Just a headache. I'll be fine."

"Daddy! Mommy!" The squeal interrupted whatever Holt had been about to say.

"Mommy?" Libby groaned.

"Don't worry, we'll get it sorted out."

The woman who held Jill smiled benignly as Holt deposited Libby on the porch. "I'll get the luggage," he said, striding off.

Libby returned the smile. The woman was tall and statuesque, giving the impression of strength overlaid with femininity. She looked to be in her early forties. A man, who was even taller but thin to the point of gauntness, nodded quickly at Libby and followed Holt. Two other children watched from the doorway.

Jill stretched out her hands to be taken, and Libby automatically responded, lifting her from the woman's arms. The child looked too pleased with herself.

Libby decided to take the bull by the horns. She shifted Jill to one hip and extended her hand. "Hello, I'm Libby Hamilton, a good friend of the Whitneys. It's very kind of you to help us out like this."

Jill's face fell. The woman looked confused as she returned the handshake. "You're not Jill's mother?" she asked.

Jill buried her face in Libby's neck.

She knew the child was embarrassed at being caught in a lie, and she didn't want to hurt her. On the other hand, the situation had to be clarified. "No," Libby said, fondly ruffling the child's hair. "But she's a darling. I wish I had a little girl just like her."

The woman opened her mouth to voice her surprise, then evidently changed her mind. The benign smile turned to one of genuine friendliness. "I'm Dixie Gartland. Come in, come in. I don't know what I'm thinking of, letting you stand out here in the freezing cold like this." She rubbed her sweater-clad arms and led the way into the house. "These are our daughters, Carrie and Sue," she said, closing the door behind them. "There's a fire in the parlor. This way."

As they all trooped after her, Libby spoke to the two little girls. The elder, Carrie, was probably six or seven, while the younger looked to be Jill's age. "How do you do?" they chorused, their piping voices as identical as their excited smiles. Jill wiggled to get down, and they each took one of her hands.

The parlor was one of two that flanked the wide entrance hall. A very old organ, polished until the wood gleamed like a mirror, stood against one wall, a large TV against another. Twin sofas faced each other in front of the busy fireplace. They were upholstered in blue and wonderfully puffy and soft looking. Evidently Dixie had chosen to forgo stiff Victorian authenticity for comfort.

"What a lovely home you have. And how very kind of you to take us in," Libby said, sinking into the cushions.

Dixie shrugged. "In the country you get used to helping out in an emergency. This storm certainly qualifies. I'm just glad your, uh, Mr. Whitney was able to find you. Here, let me take your coat."

Libby gave it up willingly. Cozy firelight warmed the room, augmented by the soft glow of kerosene lamps. "So am I." She shuddered, remembering. "I was terrified. I had run my car off the road and into a ditch," she added in a husky voice.

"My God," whispered Dixie in genuine horror. "You could have died. And look at that bruise. Come, sit by the fire," she urged.

Libby gratefully moved closer to the warmth and touched her temple. "The bruise must look worse than it feels. I'm fine now, really."

They heard the two men returning, stomping their booted feet at the front door, dropping luggage and conversing in undertones. Both women looked toward the hall.

Libby felt her breath grow shallow when she saw Holt enter the parlor.

Holt came to stand by Libby's side at the fireplace, meeting her eyes with a tender smile. "Okay?" he asked softly. "Did you get some aspirin?"

"They're in my purse."

Dixie sent her older daughter for a glass of water, and Holt retrieved the purse. When she returned, he took the glass from the child. His hand curved around Libby's fingers on the glass, and his gaze locked on hers as she swallowed the tablets.

Libby was too bemused to object.

"I don't have school tomorrow," said Carrie.

"Neither do I," added Sue.

"Silly," said her older sister scornfully. "You don't even go to school."

"Well," reasoned the child, "if I did, I wouldn't have to go tomorrow." She turned to look up at Libby. "Our lights are out."

"I noticed." Libby hid a smile. "But aren't the lanterns pretty?"

Dixie interrupted, displaying for the first time her organizational ability. "Miss Hamilton, this is my husband, Tom. Girls, go in and set the table while I show our guests to their rooms. Take Jill with you. Tom, help Mr. Whitney with the bags." She was waving her hands, shooing them in the directions she wanted them to take. "This formality is silly. Miss Hamilton, Mr. Whitney...what is your first name?" she asked Holt.

Grinning, Holt guided Libby with a hand at her back. "Holt," he answered easily.

"Fine," she said, sailing out of the room like the Pied Piper with all of them trailing behind. They were met at the foot of the stairs by yet another Gartland, Tommy, a seventeen-year-old who was nearly as tall as his father.

"Don't shake his hand," Dixie ordered. "He's been in the barn. There's no telling what's on it. Tommy, you get cleaned up for dinner."

"Yes, ma'am."

It occurred to Libby that those were the first words she'd heard a male member of the Gartland family utter.

WITH AN UNMISTAKABLE ATTEMPT at nonchalance, Dixie spoke. "Here are the two rooms. I don't know how you'll want to arrange yourselves." She threw open the door to a bedroom that was charmingly decorated around a huge, old-fashioned canopy bed. White eyelet ruffles edged the canopy and spread, which were a warm shade of rose. Rose drapes were loosely tied back at the windows, and a lighter shade of the color carpeted the floor. Two easy chairs in forest green were drawn up in front of a small fireplace, where a coal fire simmered cheerfully in the grate. Despite the size of the bed it was definitely a woman's room, from the silver appointments on the dresser to the frilly lampshade on the bedside table.

"This looks like a good spot for Libby," Holt said immediately, earning himself a figurative pat on the head and a smile from their hostess. He set Libby's two suitcases down beside the bed.

Libby guessed Dixie wouldn't have said a word about their sleeping arrangements, but she was obviously conservative about such things and found her relief hard to hide.

The next moment, however, the older woman was inspecting Holt's big frame with an expression that bordered on the droll. "You'd better wait until you see the next one," she said wryly. Opening a connecting door, she indicated that they should inspect the room beyond. "I'll get you all some towels." She left them alone.

This room had obviously once been used as a nursery, for the only door was the one they stood in. The floor was bare except for small throw rugs, the glow from the fireplace reflected on polished oak. There were twin beds, but they appeared to be youth length, beautifully covered in quilted ecru linen, but small even compared to an ordinary bed. Holt eyed them with barely hidden dismay.

Libby came to a sudden decision. "I'll share this with Jill."

Holt smiled his gratitude, then moved her hair aside and began to rub the tight muscles in her neck with careful pressure. "How's your headache?"

"Ah, that feels good," said Libby, closing her eyes and leaning into the soothing massage. "The aspirin helped. Thanks."

"Jill isn't your responsibility, Libby. Are you sure you don't mind sleeping in here?" Holt kept his voice low.

"There isn't as much of me as there is of you; besides, I can just picture you in all those ruffles." She opened her eyes again and indicated the room behind them with a tilt of her head and a grin. "The sight would be too good to miss."

"You could always join me there if you felt cramped," he offered with a chuckle of masculine anticipation.

"And shock our hostess?" She lifted her brows in mock horror.

His hand ceased its massage, making a restless movement along her spine. "Would you consider it, otherwise?" he asked, suddenly husky voiced and dark eyed and totally serious.

"You folks want to sort this out?" Tom stood in the doorway to the hall, holding a suitcase in each large hand and one tucked under his arm.

Libby was grateful to the man. At that moment she had no idea what her answer to Holt would have been. After the scene in the van, her feelings had undergone a drastic change. She was just as attracted to him as before, but her inclination to deny those feelings was definitely diminishing.

"Thanks, Tom," said Holt.

"Dixie will have supper ready in a few minutes. She said to show you the bathroom. It's right through here."

The bath was off the larger bedroom, meaning that Jill and Libby would have to go through whenever they needed to use it. *Oh, well,* thought Libby with a sigh, *it's better than his coming through my bedroom unexpectedly. And infinitely better than freezing to death on the side of Interstate 65.*

Jill followed Tom into the room. She was delighted with the sleeping arrangements. She climbed onto the other twin bed and chattered as Holt separated the luggage and Libby unpacked what she would need for the night. "We can talk after we're in bed, like Carrie and Sue," she told Libby.

"Is that what they do?"

"Yes." The child nodded. "And sometimes they put a light under the covers and look at books. You ought to see their room, Libby, it's this big." She spread her arms to show the biggest thing her mind could imagine.

"Hey, squirt," came her daddy's voice from the doorway.

He was speaking to his daughter but looking at Libby. Her throat grew dry at the expression of desire that Tom's interruption had done nothing to cool. His gaze dropped to her hands and she realized she was holding her nightgown, a frothy scrap of a thing. She dropped it immediately and turned away. This afternoon's near tragedy had broken down the barriers between them.

Holt swallowed uncomfortably. "Come wash your hands before dinner, Jill."

"Okay," she agreed reluctantly. "Don't Libby have to wash up, too?"

"Doesn't," Holt corrected. "Come on."

Jill seemed to sense something was going on between the adults that she didn't understand. She straightened, following her father out of the room.

Sinking onto the bed, Libby sighed with relief. Holt simply had to look at her like that, with hunger burning free behind the polished facade he normally wore, and she was weakened to the point of surrender.

She could hear the two of them moving around in the next room. Jill's childish soprano chatter was punctuated by Holt's baritone. Finally, all was quiet and Libby rose, intending to wash her own flushed face with cold water before going downstairs.

Once again he filled the doorway, his palms flattened on either side of the jamb. The casual stance stretched his shirt across the muscles of his chest. One leg was cocked in a deceptively casual position that emphasized his lean hips and strong thighs. "Bathroom's free," he said easily.

"Thanks." The word didn't come out right, and she cleared her throat to untangle her voice. "Thanks," she said, more forcefully. She approached him, hoping he would move aside but not really expecting it. When she was less than three feet away, she halted. She tilted her head to one side and gave him a half smile. "Are you going to let me by, or am I going to have to hurt you?"

His laugh was one of pure pleasure. With a swoop of one arm he caught her around the waist to drag her against him.

She yelped. "Holt! Don't do that."

He held her, feet barely touching the floor, with her mouth only inches from his. "Will you come into my room tonight, Libby?"

"No." She squirmed to be free.

"To talk, Libby, only to talk," he assured her earnestly.

"Why do I have trouble believing you?" she said with a snort.

"I swear," he murmured, his lips drawing closer. Suddenly she realized the teasing tone was gone from his voice. "We need to have a talk, without Jill, without anyone else around. Just each other. Don't you think so, Libby?"

The way he said her name filled her mind with images, of the two of them, naked and glowing after the exertion of making love. She turned slightly away to hide the expression of arousal in her eyes. The scent of him, masculine and spicy, filled her nostrils, traveled quickly to her brain, erasing with an efficient swipe all her common sense.

She agreed with him about the need to communicate. Through circumstance, fate—whatever—they were more than two people who had met by chance, briefly, never to see each other again. Slowly and carefully, she laid her cheek on his shoulder.

Holt tucked his chin to look down at the woman held so securely against his body. He felt a rush of such warmth and desire that it took his breath away. His eyes closed for an instant, as he remembered his frantic fear this afternoon when he hadn't been able to find her. The bleakness of the howling snowstorm was nothing compared to the bleak feeling that he had lost a part of himself. One minute, he had faced the task of fitting a daughter into his life with a minimum of fuss, the next he faced an involvement that he accepted but wasn't sure he welcomed.

So much for not getting involved. He had a feeling he would always be involved with Libby, whether anything permanent came of their relationship or not. Even if he could bring himself to say goodbye again, that wouldn't be enough. She would live with him forever in his memory.

He wrapped his other arm around her, lowering his head. His lips brushed the downy softness of her cheek. Her lashes fluttered, and he kissed them shut once more. Desire ebbed, to be replaced by an awesome, almost reverent tenderness. They would have time for passion—he knew that instinctively—but he recognized that the warmer, tender feeling was special, one he wasn't familiar with but one he was willing to savor for the moment.

The sound of running, coming from several pairs of feet, interrupted his contentment. He lifted his head, listening. His arms contracted.

Libby empathized with Holt's reluctance to release her and looked up at him with a tender smile.

"What's there to smile about?" he growled softly.

She was struck anew by the beautiful blue color of his eyes, even filled with frustration as they were. "Nothing, I guess," she whispered.

"Damn right." He let her regain her footing before he released her. "Can we talk later, in my room?" He had stepped back. Now his stance was defensive, as though the gentle emotion he'd felt was disconcerting.

He was as unsure of these new feelings as she was, Libby realized with surprise. She took a long breath. "You're sure, of course, that all you want to do is talk?" she teased unsteadily, and saw his body relax.

Jill came bursting into the room with Sue on her heels. "Supper's ready. Hurry, Daddy, I'm hungry."

"We're on our way," Holt said to the girls, and then turned back to answer Libby's question with a hypothetical one. "In this house full of people?" he drawled. His grin spread to disperse the remaining frustration. "We might neck a little, but it won't get serious."

Libby choked on her laughter. "You—you go on downstairs with the children. I'll be right there."

"You haven't washed your hands *yet?*" asked Jill.

DINNER, OR SUPPER, as the Gartlands called their evening meal, consisted of hot corn bread, salad and a beef-laden stew with chunks of potato, carrot and onion. Dixie and Tom sat at opposite ends of the large dining-room table, with Holt, Jill and Carrie on one side and Tommy, Sue and Libby along the other.

"Thank goodness we have a gas stove." Dixie was answering Libby's question about how she'd prepared such a meal under the circumstances. "And all the rooms have fireplaces. We've survived these storms before in relative comfort." Her expression sobered. "It's the poor animals we have to worry about if the snow stays on the ground for long."

"I don't guess you have to worry much about weather in Florida, do you, Holt?" her husband asked.

"Not for my cattle, Tom, but I have a nice-sized orange grove, and the citrus industry has been through three really bad years."

Tom nodded. There ensued a discussion of farming and cattle. Libby watched the man across the table and wondered what would be said between them later. At one point in their conversation Holt stopped eating to lean forward, listening with respect to Tom's comments. He also spoke with authority, and she noticed the older man deferring to him on a number of subjects, as well.

It occurred to her, from an objective viewpoint, that Holt Whitney was a many-faceted person, and the more facets she discovered, the more intrigued she was.

She looked away once to find Dixie watching her with a quizzical gleam in her eye. She smiled weakly. Dixie toasted her with her coffee cup.

Jill finally had enough of not being the center of attention. She began to whine and, when the older Carrie tried to soothe her with a pat on the shoulder and the promise of dessert, she twisted away from her hand, upsetting her milk and bursting into tears.

Holt immediately righted the glass and began mopping at the spilled milk with his napkin. "I'm really sorry, Dixie," he said over his daughter's sobs.

"Don't worry. It certainly isn't the first glass of milk that's been spilled at this table, and I'm sure it won't be the last." Once again the general took charge. She rose to begin clearing the table. "Carrie, you get a towel from the kitchen. Tommy, bring in the dessert. These little ones have had a long day; they need to be in bed."

Libby, accustomed to a large family where everyone pitched in, collected Tom's plate along with her own and carried them into the kitchen.

Holt picked up Jill and cuddled her on his lap. "Shh, sweetheart. It's all right," he murmured, wondering if it was a law of nature that grown men should be turned to mush at the sight of a woman's tears, no matter what her age.

Soon the tears slowed, and she popped a thumb into her mouth. She looked up at him. "Am I going to get a spanking?" she asked tremulously around her thumb.

He smiled. "Do you think you need one?" he teased.

To his surprise, she nodded. "I was a bad girl."

He wasn't sure how to handle the situation. If he disagreed with her, he was saying it was okay to throw a tantrum; if he agreed, he might be right back where they'd been two days before they'd left Chicago, when his daughter had submitted to his direction like a trained monkey but barely spoke to him. Damn Linda!

Oh, hell, that wasn't fair, either. Linda had done her best...he supposed. The child psychologist hadn't prepared him for this one. Well, all he could do was what felt right, and it felt right to soothe instead of scold. "You're tired, sweetheart. You didn't mean to turn over your milk." He hugged the small body. "Now, how about some dessert?" he suggested cheerfully.

Jill frowned at him. "I want to go to bed," she said firmly.

"Bed?" He didn't think kids ever *wanted* to go to bed, but he shrugged and stood with her in his arms. "Jill is tired," he told the others. "She wants to go to bed."

Sue looked at her contemporary as though Jill had some strange disease. "I don't," she told her mother quickly.

Dixie hid a smile. "Okay. Good night, Jill. We'll see you in the morning."

"'Night," Jill said softly over her father's shoulder as he carried her out of the room.

Dixie met Libby's eyes with a knowing smile. She began to cut and serve the lemon-meringue pie. "He consulted a psychiatrist, you say?"

Libby had given her a capsulized history while they were in the kitchen. She nodded.

"You being from a large family yourself, maybe you can help him. He has an education in store over the next few months." She passed a plate to Tommy, who in turn handed it to Libby.

Libby stiffened at the assumption. "I probably won't see that much of them when we get to Florida."

Dixie didn't answer, but her eyes clearly reflected her disbelief.

When Holt returned to the table a few minutes later, the conversation had switched to the weather. After dinner the adults took their coffee cups into Tom's study to listen to the forecast on his portable radio. The storm was moving slowly from the Mississippi Valley toward the Atlantic seaboard. The main highways were expected to be cleared by late tomorrow afternoon.

"We're not far from Nashville," Holt told Libby as they mounted the stairs later. "Tomorrow I'll call the dealership there and see about having your car towed."

Libby took a long breath. "I can take care of it," she said shortly. "I told you, I don't need caring for."

"Oh?" he queried with a hint of sarcasm.

Too late she realized she'd put her foot neatly into her mouth. "This morning—afternoon—was stupidity, not vulnerability," she admitted wryly.

Holt held the door to the bedroom for her. "Same result. You got yourself into one hell of a lot of trouble, didn't you? The fire's dying down," he observed, switching topics without even a pause for breath. "I'd better check the one in your room."

"I'll do it."

"You promised me talk, remember? Sit down. I'll be right back."

Libby was suddenly too nervous to sit. The importance of the deferred talk had been forgotten during dinner, but now, in this cozy firelit room, the talk took on gigantic proportions. Her chin came up defensively. She needed bright light to dispel the romantic atmosphere. She strode across to the switch on the wall beside the door. Not until she had flicked it twice and looked at it rather blankly, did she remember there was no power. "Damn," she muttered under her breath, and returned to stand in front of the fireplace.

"Did you say something?"

She turned from the blaze to glance over her shoulder. "Is Jill asleep?"

"Out like a log."

"Holt, I'm tired, too." The lie slipped from her lips as easily as the fake smile. She had never felt so wide awake in her life. "I think I'll go to bed."

"Coward," he accused softly as he came from behind her to slide his arms around her waist.

"Yes, I know," she admitted, tilting her head to give him more room to nuzzle her neck. "But you said we'd talk, and I have a feeling we're not going to do much of that."

"Honey, I know I'm rushing you," he said between nibbles. "But you're not resisting very hard."

"That's what bothers me."

He turned her in his arms and, taking hold of her shoulders, walked her backward until she felt the chair at her knees. She sat at the urging of his hands. He leaned down to leave a kiss at her temple before sitting in the chair at her side. "I do want to talk, Libby. I want to learn all about you. Tell me more about your family."

She laid her head against the back of her chair and stared into the fire. "I've already told you about them. They are loving, warm...."

"And they smother you," he finished for her. "Why?"

"They don't realize what they're doing." She sighed. "I was their 'baby.'"

Holt didn't make a sound, and soon she was lost in her memories. He reached over to link their fingers lightly.

She smiled at him gratefully, then looked beyond into the fire with a thoughtful expression. "It isn't easy being the baby. You know, if someone else is willing to do everything for you, it's very easy to get in the habit of not doing things for yourself. That's the danger. For a long time I was content to let the others take responsibility for me. Anyway, by the time I finished high school I was spoiled rotten. I lived at home for the first two years of college. They gave me money when my allowance ran out, often when they couldn't afford it."

Holt's fingers tightened. The admission confirmed that there was much more to this woman than her looks and sex appeal.

"I still feel guilty about that, and sorry, because I just reinforced their opinion that I couldn't take care of myself. I finally grew up when I was twenty. I moved into an apartment for my last two years of college and tried to get my life on course." Libby smiled reminiscently. "Having my own place helped, but I finally realized it hadn't solved the problem completely. At some point they decided I needed to be married. Over the next few years, friends, uncles, cousins, brothers, nephews were all introduced with blatant hints. And every time my family came up with another candidate, I'd dig my heels in harder.

"Then about six months ago, I got engaged to a friend of my brother, a thoroughly nice man. The engagement lasted three months. I broke it off when I realized he was an extension of my family. His sole purpose in life would have been to take care of me."

Holt made an inarticulate sound. She wasn't interested in being tied down. Why wasn't he pleased by that knowledge?

"What? Did you say something?"

"No, go on."

"There isn't much more. On the day he told me I could keep my 'little job' until I got pregnant, I knew it wasn't going to work. I finally woke up to the fact that I needed to be away, on my own. So when the opportunity for this job came up, I took it. I feel guilty as hell. The disruption my exodus stirred up..." She shook her head.

"What about the men? Wasn't there ever anyone else you felt serious about?"

"No. I'm not saying there couldn't have been." She laughed stiffly after a minute. "But by then, the resistance was ingrained." The truth was that she yearned for freedom. Maybe in a few years she might want a permanent relationship. Maybe someday, but not now.

"What are you looking for, Libby?" Holt asked quietly. "More than independence, I think."

"I'm not sure," she answered, concealing the thoughts that related to him. "A chance to be myself, I guess. To prove I have some worth." Her eyes were dark with appeal as she turned her head against the chair, her eyes meeting his.

"Of course you have worth. You're being too harsh with your family. Families are like that...if they're close and care." The last was added after a pause.

"Maybe I am being too harsh, but I can't help how I feel. I have to deal with my life the only way I can."

He gave her that lazy smile. "Maybe your youthful look is part of your problem. A few gray hairs and you're home free." He sat forward in his chair and reached for the poker to stir the coals. The action stretched his shirt tight across his muscular shoulders.

Libby curled her fingers into her palm to still the urge to run her hand over his back. The warmth of the fire, the relaxation after a tension-filled day, the pleasurable intimacy in the room—all converged to induce a lethargic reverie that stole her remaining energy. She felt boneless.

"I hesitate to mention this, but I think you have a more immediate problem." He smiled over his shoulder with something akin to an apology in his eyes. "Are you supposed to stay in contact with your family?"

"Oh, Lord, yes!" She sat straight up in her chair. "What will they think when they hear the weather report? I have to call them."

"Honey, the phone isn't working," Holt reminded her. He smiled to himself. She might have left under strained circumstances, but her family's feelings were still of major concern. Some time, distance, and she would be able to accept their love without resentment. And they might realize their baby was a capable, intelligent woman with a mind of her own.

She subsided against the cushion. "Oh, dear."

"Do you think your brothers will be coming after me with a snowplow?"

She smiled, pretending to assess his chances as she eyed him from top to toes. "You're bigger than they are," she said at last. "Besides, you're a father. If there's anything they love, it's children."

"And you? How do you feel about children?" Holt watched for a reaction. For the first time in her life Libby was free to be herself, to make her own decisions. Why would she want to get involved with a man who already had enough responsibilities? Hell! For that matter, why would a man with those responsibilities want to get involved, either, at least not until he had his own life straightened out. But as he looked at the woman beside him, he knew he was already dependent on her, whether he wanted to be or not.

Maybe the fear he had experienced had brought this on. Since the breakup of his marriage he had avoided obligation, and now here he was thinking in terms of permanence with a woman he'd known for two days.

Libby Hamilton might have been a spoiled brat when she was eighteen—though he doubted she had been as bad as she thought—but now she was as loving and giving a person as he'd ever known.

Holt didn't like to rely on another for his peace of mind, either. He had been that route once, the happily-ever-after route that turned out to be happily until the big career came along. Now, he had his daughter. Getting the two of them settled into some kind of harmonious relationship was going to take all his energy for a while.

Yet fate had stepped in, presenting him with a woman who would be impossible to say goodbye to. He wanted her physically, but there was also another, deeper void in him...she filled so easily and naturally that it scared him to death. Of course, he would be drawn to a woman who was no more interested in settling down with a family than his wife had been.

Holt looked across at her and almost laughed out loud. She was slouched in the chair sound asleep, her head at an angle that he knew was uncomfortable. With a half smile, he let his gaze roam over her face, the thick fan of lashes that shadowed her cheeks in the firelight, the full lower lip that was so soft, tasted so sweet, her long slender neck and her breasts formed so perfectly.

Desire surged through his body with a force that shocked him. He squirmed uncomfortably against the sudden restriction of his jeans. Lord! He was going to have to get her out of his bedroom before he was tempted to strip her and throw her onto the bed. Tempted, hell! He craved her.

He stood abruptly, took a few steps and more than a few deep breaths, and returned to stand in front of her. "Libby." His voice came out hoarse and hesitant. He cleared his throat and tried again. "Libby."

For an instant, a split second when she opened her eyes, he saw the emotion she couldn't hide, and his heart leaped joyously. He hunkered down, fencing her in with a hand on each of the chair arms. "Honey," he said very softly, "you're exhausted. You'd better go to bed."

She smiled, alerting the dimple in her cheek, and he caught his breath. Using his hands for leverage he leaned forward, drawn as though on a string to cover her smile very carefully with his lips. The moment was too full, too deep with feeling. Deliberately, hoping to lighten it, he lifted a suggestive brow. "Do you need any help getting ready for bed?" he asked with a grin.

Libby tried to hide her disappointment. When she had opened her eyes to see his tender, loving expression she had thought dreamily that somehow, without her knowing, they had moved along to another plane in their relationship. Despite her resolve, her promises to herself, at that moment she was filled with excitement at the prospect.

She must have misread the message in his eyes, because now the only emotion in their blue depths was a teasing glimmer of affection.

6

LIBBY AWOKE THE NEXT MORNING to soft kisses dropping over her forehead and eyes. The covers reaching halfway up her face were pulled down below her chin. "There you are." A husky whisper fanned her lashes. "You really bury yourself in the covers, don't you?"

Holt, she thought, taking a deep satisfied breath. Clean smells—soap, spicy after-shave, minty toothpaste—tickled her nostrils. She sighed and opened her mouth to speak.

"Shh. Jill's asleep," came the whisper again, and then she was being lifted with an arm beneath her shoulders. Her lips were smothered by a hungry early-morning kiss.

It was a wonderful way to wake up, Libby decided. She worked her arms free of the sheet and blanket and wound them loosely, drowsily around the broad shoulders above her. Her tactile exploration told her he had on a shirt starched lightly at the collar and a sweater knitted of some wonderfully soft yarn. She combed the fingers of one hand through his still-damp hair. "Mmm, you've already showered. You smell good." She smiled contentedly, her eyes still closed.

"So do you, warm and sweet and sexy as hell. Open your eyes. I want to make sure you know who's holding you."

"I know," she murmured. She opened them, anyway. His face was only a breath away, and the expression there threatened to stop her heart.

The lazy half smile he habitually wore was in place, but in contrast his eyes burned with longing.

"Holt," she murmured hesitantly.

"Do you know how very much I want you right this minute?" he groaned softly. "You look so beautiful with your eyes smoky and sleepy, your mouth uncolored, your hair all wild and tangled, like an angel who's got a streak of the devil in her." Suddenly he lifted her across his lap, covers and all, and buried his face in the soft skin of her throat. He stripped the sheet and blanket to her waist and cupped her full breast through her gown, his fingers stroking over the tip until it responded, pouting into his palm.

She wanted him, too, she thought dazedly, wanted the weight of his muscular body pressing down on her, wanted to feel his hands and mouth on her bare skin. Instinctively she shifted her hips, feeling the thrust of his arousal against her thigh. He lifted his head, the fire in his eyes now out of control. His mouth came crashing down, abrasive against her lips, but she didn't care. She returned the rough kiss fiercely, demanding as much as he demanded.

"I have to go to the bathroom." The small voice shot through the charged atmosphere like a bolt of lightning, dividing them effectively into two separate bodies again. Libby found herself dumped unceremoniously back on the bed. Holt stood abruptly.

Jill was sitting cross-legged in the middle of her bed, watching them curiously. "What are you doing?" she asked.

Letting go of a gasp, Libby leaned back against the pillow, pulling the covers up to her nose as she watched Holt's ears turn a brilliant shade of red. She caught her lower lip between her teeth to keep from laughing at his expression. The laugh would certainly have held a note of hysteria.

Taking a ragged breath, he shoved his hands into the pockets of his jeans and looked to her for support. She shrugged helplessly but found herself gleefully anticipating the show.

"We were kissing," he told Jill bluntly.

Libby could have hoped for more diplomacy, but she supposed under the circumstances the answer was adequate.

"Why were you pinching Libby's chest?"

Libby shut her eyes and bit down hard on the blanket, but she couldn't control the choking sound. Holt glared at her, his indigo eyes promising retribution at the first opportunity. "Was I doing that?" he asked his daughter innocently. "I didn't notice. Why don't you run on to the bathroom? I'll be there in a minute."

"Okay." As Jill slid off the bed and padded toward the door, Libby flopped onto her stomach, burying her face in the pillow to muffle the laughter she could no longer contain.

A large fist caught most of her hair and turned her head. Her body had to follow. The rest of her giggles were swallowed by a brief hard kiss. "You were a hell of a lot of help," he accused with a grin.

"I know. I'm sorry. Bu-but if you could have seen your face..." She went off into more peals of laughter. And naturally he had to quiet her with another leisurely kiss.

When the amusement had finally subsided in both of them, Holt raised his head to look tenderly into her eyes. His elbows were planted on either side of her head, and his fingers played with the loose curls spread across the pillow. "You're different from any woman I've ever known," he said in a low voice.

"Am I? How?"

He frowned and shook his head slightly. "I'm not sure I could put it into words."

Smiling, she brought both hands up to cradle his face, her thumb investigating the dimple in his cheek. "Try," she urged softly.

"Libby Hamilton, I think I could fall in love with you without much trouble at all."

She stiffened at the declaration. "No, Holt, don't spoil it. You must know I'm not ready for anything this serious."

He went on as though she hadn't spoken. "Yesterday. . ." He shuddered. "When I thought you were lost..." His face twisted in remembered pain.

"Shh." She relaxed, soothing him despite her wariness, bringing his head down to her neck and wrapping her arms tightly around his neck. This man had saved her life. How could she deny him her warmth? "It's over now. You found me. It's all over."

"Are you kissing *again*?" said the disgusted voice from only inches away. This time they both turned their heads slowly. Jill's chin was propped on her crossed arms at the edge of the bed.

"Yep," said her father. "Does it bother you to see us kissing?"

The child considered a moment. "I don't guess so, if you like it." Her tone said clearly that she couldn't understand the appeal. "Is it still snowing?"

"Just a little." Holt reached out to lift her onto the bed, into the circle of their embrace. She snuggled contentedly between them.

Libby reached out, too. Her hand encountered the child's bare fanny, so that she lifted her head in surprise. "Jill Whitney, what happened to the bottom half of your pajamas? Come here under the covers before you freeze." Actually the room was cool but not uncomfortably cold. Holt must have built up the fire this morning before he'd woken her.

"I didn't see why I should put them back on when it's time to get dressed," Jill answered reasonably, squirming into the warm cave Libby made by lifting a corner of the blanket.

Libby chuckled. "You're absolutely right," she said, hugging the child. "I'll help you dress if you think you can get rid of your daddy for a few minutes."

When they turned as one to look at Holt, they were both surprised at the expression on his face. He looked stunned, his cheeks almost drained of color.

"Holt?"

"Daddy?" said Jill. "What's the matter?"

"Nothing, sweetheart. Not a thing." Holt tightened his arms around them in a quick convulsive clasp and then almost leaped up from the bed. "I'll leave you to dress," he said huskily.

WHEN LIBBY CAME DOWNSTAIRS with Jill a short while later she wore a denim skirt and a red gingham shirt with a red crew-neck sweater. Jill wore denim overalls with a red gingham shirt and a red cardigan sweater, all of which had been buried at the bottom of her suitcase but which she insisted on digging out so they would match.

The child was growing too attached to her, Libby realized, through no fault of Holt's. He took full responsibility for Jill. The fault lay with her. No more offering to help Jill dress, she resolved. No more taking the traditional woman's role when faced with a child. It wasn't fair to Holt or Jill. She was certain that was what had put the unreadable expression in Holt's eyes before he'd left them. He was just getting to know his daughter. Libby felt guilty, monopolizing the child's affection when Holt had been deprived of his daughter for so long.

Carrie and Sue met them at the bottom of the stairs. "C'mon, Jill!" they cried. "You have to eat your breakfast! Your daddy's going to help us build a snowman as soon as you're finished!" They each took a hand and dragged the younger girl off between them.

Libby followed them through the hall to the swinging door of the kitchen, where Carrie had already helped Jill scramble onto a chair and arranged a napkin in her lap. "Now eat," she ordered, hopping up into her own chair beside her sister.

Grinning, Holt poured a mug of steaming coffee for Libby, handing it to her while Dixie scolded her older daughter. "Carrie, you don't rush someone through their meal. She'll get indigestion, poor mite. Mornin', Libby."

"Good morning, Dixie."

The kitchen was as warm as toast and cozily crowded. The two male members of the Gartland family sat at the round table before the bay window. They nodded a hello and resumed eating.

"I hope you two don't mind waiting until somebody's through. This table won't hold as many as the one in the dining room, but we let the fire go out in there last night."

Tom Gartland finished first. He wiped his mouth with his napkin and stood up. "Hurry up, Tommy," he told his son. "Got to get to work."

"I'll be out to lend a hand, Tom," Holt said quietly.

Tom turned with the first genuine grin Libby'd seen him give. "Appreciate the offer, but not until you finish with the snowman. Can't think how you let yourself get talked into that. I hate the things myself." He took his coat and hat off a hook near the back door and went outside, to be followed shortly by his son.

When breakfast was finally over, Libby was left alone in the kitchen with Dixie. They worked in companionable silence, Dixie washing, Libby drying the dishes.

The snow hadn't stopped completely, but that didn't deter the three younger children. Their laughter drifted on the cold air to penetrate the house. Libby gazed through the window, an absent smile on her lips, her thoughts focused on the kiss she and Holt had shared that morning. A sultry slow-motion replay blunted her consciousness when she recalled the feel of his hand on her breast. Longing and urgency for physical fulfillment with this man were building within her to a dangerous degree, but the need wasn't only physical. She would be a fool not to admit she could very easily fall in love with him.

"How long have you known each other?" Dixie asked as she squeezed out the dishcloth and hung it inside the cabinet below the sink. Her head disappeared after it as she reached for something deep inside.

Libby sliced a look of pure mischief at her back. She folded the towel neatly. Crossing her arms, she leaned a hip against the edge of the counter. "Three days," she said casually.

Dixie's head came up with a jerk. Libby heard the bump against the cabinet. "Ouch!"

"Oh, Dixie!" Libby grabbed her arm to help her to her feet. "I'm sorry. I shouldn't have sprung it on you like that. Are you hurt?"

Though she rubbed the spot, she denied any damage. "I'm okay. Three days! You must be a fast worker."

Libby looked at her blankly. "Fast worker? What do you mean?"

"I mean the man is crazy about you. It's so obvious even Tom noticed," Dixie added wryly.

Libby turned away to hide her smile of delight. "He's just grateful that I'm good with kids," she demurred.

"Libby, I'm not blind. The electricity between you could light up this house even with the power off." Her voice dropped to a low sympathetic level. "And, honey, when he first arrived with Jill, when he didn't know whether you were safe or not, he was wild with fear. I've never seen a man so frantic."

Libby's jaw dropped. Worried, yes, but she couldn't imagine Holt being frantic.

"That's why I assumed you were married, that and the fact that Jill called you Mommy. What happened— No! Never mind. I'm just being nosy."

Libby smiled at the older woman's curiosity. "I don't think Holt would mind your knowing. You've been so wonderful to us.... Jill's mother lives in Chicago. She's an actress. I gather the child has spent a lot of time with an older woman, a nurse, who finally had to retire. Holt was concerned about her and finally got his ex-wife to agree to give him custody."

"Poor child. She probably doesn't even know who her mother is." Dixie's mouth drooped sadly.

Libby laughed. "I don't think that's the case. Holt doesn't seem to harbor any ill feelings toward his ex-wife. And I'm sure he would if she had neglected the child."

"Hmm. Yes, you're right. He would be furious. I wonder what happened to split them up," she added with an attempt at nonchalance.

"I wouldn't presume to speculate," answered Libby firmly. She knew part of the story but, aside from the fact that Holt definitely would object to her discussing his former marriage, any thought of him with his wife caused pangs in the region of her heart. She didn't want to think about it, much less discuss it.

"Do you think it's beginning to snow harder?" she asked, leaning forward to peer out of the window.

Dixie joined her. "Looks that way. They're going to be frozen when they come inside. I'd better make a pot of cocoa." She smiled indulgently. "I love snow for Christmas, but it sure makes a lot of extra work."

"Can I do anything?"

Dixie looked around her kitchen. "I've finished most of the baking, but I did want to make ambrosia today. If you could keep the children occupied for a while, that would help."

"Sure, I can do that," Libby agreed cheerfully.

"Tonight, we'll put up the tree and decorate. It's a good thing I'm an early shopper."

Talk about Christmas plans and shopping and decorating sent Libby's thoughts winging north. Her family's tree was never decorated until after the children were in bed on Christmas Eve. It always appeared as though by magic on Christmas morning. Even now that the five of them were grown with homes of their own, the decorating was a special task her mother and father shared. Everyone met at church on Christmas morning and returned afterward for a traditional feast. Her eyes clouded at the memories. She would miss it all this year.

"Do you mind if I try to get a weather report on Tom's radio?" she asked Dixie. Her voice came out in a croak that brought the older woman's gaze to hers.

"Not at all," she said kindly. "Bring it in here, if you like."

"My family's going to be very worried. I wish there was a way to get word to them."

"There is," said Dixie. "I told you, we've lived through enough of these storms to be prepared. If you'll write a message now, we'll put it in the mailbox out at the road and mark it with a red scarf. The people who operate the snowplows will pick it up. They can radio a message to the Chicago police."

"Thanks. I'll do it right now," she said, suddenly feeling better. "I hate for them to worry."

When she returned to the kitchen a few minutes later with her message and the portable radio, the children were back inside. Dixie was hanging wet coats over the backs of chairs, draping hats and gloves on the counter and mopping puddles of melted snow.

Libby hurried to help with little Sue and earned herself a smile from the quietest of the three children.

"Libby, Libby, did you see our snowman?" Jill launched herself at Libby's legs. "Sue and I put in the black rocks for his eyes. Daddy held us up cause the snowman's big!"

"And beautiful! I saw him through the window," she enthused, swinging the child up into her arms. "Did you have fun?"

"Yes, I did. Daddy's gone to work now, though, and I don't know what I'll do," she said woefully.

Libby joined in Dixie's laughter. "Maybe I can come up with some ideas," she offered, earning a grateful smile from Dixie.

"Thanks, Libby. It will be a big help if you can."

"Let's just hear what the weatherman has to say first," she told the children as she set the radio on the table.

The news was not good. The front that had been expected to move through by tonight had stalled, and the
forecast was conditional. "Looks as if I may be stuck
with you all for a while," Dixie said with a warmth and
cheerfulness that further endeared her to Libby.

"Yes. It's a lot of trouble...you're very kind...."

"Nonsense." Dixie gave Jill a roughly affectionate
hug. "You're no trouble at all. Are you, Jill?"

"No, I'm not trouble."

LIBBY HAD OVERESTIMATED her ability to keep three
housebound children entertained for three hours. By
lunchtime she was bewildered, dazed and praying that
the two youngest, at least, still took naps. She knew she
needed one. Caring for her nieces and nephews for an
hour or two on a pretty day hadn't prepared her for this.

Her old standby, the computer, and her supply of
games were useless without electricity. The girls were
too keyed up to settle down for a story. Indeed their energy seemed endless, and their voices would have ri-
valed NFL cheerleaders'. They weren't old enough for
card games, and they disparaged dolls. What was the
younger generation of girls coming to if they didn't like
to play dolls?

She suggested they make Christmas decorations for
their tree, but got very nervous when the girls opted for
fingerpaints and modeling clay instead. "We'd better
wait for your mother to supervise those things," she told
Carrie like the coward she was.

Carrie finally dug around in the toy box in the family room and came up with crayons. "These aren't too
messy, are they?" she asked, and Libby relented.

"I guess not." But as it turned out, for three-year-olds, keeping crayons anywhere near paper was a challenge.

She heaved a great sigh of relief when Holt came in to call them to lunch.

He took one look at her tumbled hair, her lips bare of lipstick and her wrinkled skirt and blouse and laughed. He reached down to help her up from where she was scrubbing crimson-colored wax off the polished oak floor. Wrapping his arms around her, he murmured, "Is mothering more of a job than you suspected?"

Before she could give him her wholehearted agreement, they heard snickering from the door.

"If you watch you may get to see them kiss like they did this morning," stage-whispered Jill. "And you can see my daddy—"

"Jill!" roared Holt.

Giggles erupted from all three girls.

Holt strode across the room and swept his laughing, squealing daughter up into his arms. He grinned reluctantly. "Let's go upstairs and wash your hands."

"I can wash down here," Jill protested, but not heatedly.

He tickled her, producing peals of laughter, and swiftly climbed the steps.

Despite her chagrin, Libby was moved by the teasing between father and daughter. Remembering Jill's reserve with Holt only three days ago at the truck stop, she decided his particular brand of magic worked as effectively on three-year-olds as it did on grown women.

THE SNOW HAD picked up again to blinding force, keeping the men inside after lunch. "You look a little drained," said Dixie when the last dish had been dried. "Why don't you lie down for a while?"

"Thanks, I think I will. I don't see how you do it all, Dixie. This house is huge, three children..."

"And a husband," Dixie added. "Though Tom isn't a lot of trouble." She grinned. "I guess I sort of grew into it. After all, I didn't have all of them at once."

Jill and Sue seemed almost grateful when Dixie told them that if they wanted to stay up late to help decorate the tree they had to rest. They were tired from all the physical exertion of the morning, but they would never have admitted it. "Can Jill sleep on Carrie's bed?" asked Sue.

Jill looked to Libby for permission, but Holt intervened. "I don't see why not, *if* you rest."

The children promised.

Holt went upstairs on the pretext of seeing them settled. They separated at the door to Libby's room. "Don't go to sleep yet," Holt whispered.

Libby sat on the edge of the bed to wait for him. This was as good a time as any to get a few things straight. She didn't want to be the object of more childish curiosity. They would have to be more circumspect around Jill. They were guests here, and they shouldn't behave like sex-starved teenagers, especially when the children could walk in any minute.

All of this and more she told Holt when he entered the room. She paced the floor, punctuating her remarks with her hands.

He listened silently until she finished, then stunned her by agreeing wholeheartedly.

"You do?" she asked blankly. Her hands fell limply to her sides.

He folded his arms across his chest and nodded. "I agree. We can use this time to get to know each other better, so that when I do make love to you, you won't have guilt feelings. Shall we shake on it?"

She ignored his outstretched hand. "Now, just a minute. I haven't said..."

He moved closer, laying his hands on her shoulders. His thumbs outlined her jaw and lingered to tilt her chin up. His lips curved in that familiar half smile. "We know it's going to happen sooner or later, honey," he said very softly. "Are you sure you want to argue about it right now?"

"This is as good a time as any," she told him, her chin angled defensively. She would have been able to argue better if he'd been across the room.

"Okay." He shrugged. "At least I'll have the pleasure of convincing you."

He did so very thoroughly, his kisses leaving her drowsy with desire. Finally he scooped her up in his arms and placed her gently on the bed. With a hand on each side of her head, he bent down to brush her lips one final time. "Are you convinced yet?"

"Mmm." She moistened her lips and tugged at his neck. "I'm not quite. Maybe you'd better try again."

He chuckled deep in his throat, a husky sound that told her he was as affected as she felt. "If I try again, love, I'll never stop. Sleep well."

Supper was eaten on trays in the parlor; they all took turns stringing popcorn and cranberries. "We need lots of color," Dixie directed. "If the electricity doesn't come back on, the tree won't have lights."

Sue, as the youngest, had the privilege of being lifted by her father to place the star on top of the beautiful spruce. Then the children were hustled off to bed. The grown-ups toasted the tree with Dixie's spiked eggnog.

They toasted their new friendship, they toasted the snowman, and when they started toasting the cows Dixie decided it was time to call a halt. "Let's dance," she said, tripping unsteadily to the stereo.

Tom looked at his wife with a knowing gleam in his eye.

Holt caught and interpreted the look correctly. He had to bite his cheek to keep from laughing as the older man joined his wife to whisper in her ear.

Dixie blushed and didn't quite meet Libby's eyes when Tom had led her away.

"We've decided we'll go to bed," the tall man said firmly.

Dixie giggled, and a more incongruous sound had never been heard. "Good night."

Holt pulled a laughing Libby up into his arms. He lifted her hands to his neck and pulled her against him.

"Dixie Gartland is more than a little tipsy," she observed, settling her body into the planes of his. A soft ballad from a decade ago flowed over them as they moved slowly to the rhythm.

"So is Libby Hamilton," whispered Holt into her ear. He bit lightly at the lobe, sending a chill across her shoulders, down her spine.

Libby melted against him, her steps slowing until she was barely moving. "Yes, I am. Are you going to take advantage of my weakened state?"

"Do you want me to?" His hand slid down to caress her hip through the heavy denim, then moved to the small of her back, bringing her into closer contact with his hard arousal. The friction of the stiff fabric against the fragile nylon of her panty hose produced an unexpectedly erotic sensation.

She tilted her head to look up at him. Her fingers combed through his dark hair, lifting the strands and letting them fall again. Her lips curved into a tempting smile. Her lashes descended until they screened the silver glint in her eyes. "Do you want to?"

"Golden girl, I thought you were smarter than you are if you have to ask such a question." His voice was more than a whisper, less than a murmur. He stopped dancing, if indeed that was what they had been doing. Raising his hands to cradle her head, he covered her face with kisses as soft as down, her eyelids, her brows, her cheekbones. His tongue dipped into the curve of her smile and withdrew, only to return to tease the flesh beneath her upper lip. He sipped and nibbled and kissed until she was breathing in gasps and turning her head, blindly seeking a harder pressure.

"I do," he grated. "I do want you, you devil, and you know it. But you're half-asleep." His hands tightened, raked into her hair and drew her up for the hard kiss she wanted. His tongue sought the darkest, most secret recesses of her mouth and explored and tasted until she knew his flavor as well as she knew her own.

She wanted him, too, Libby thought vaguely, and had no intention of halting this glorious experience; so when Holt pushed her away, she was confused and disconcerted. He held her by the shoulders while she looked at him through desire-blurred eyes.

"Not here," he groaned softly. "We can't make love here. Though how we're going to wait, God only knows."

THE STORM RAGED ON for two more days, while inside the comfortable house the Gartlands continued to make Libby, Holt and Jill as welcome as members of the family.

By the time the roads were cleared, the van packed and they were ready to leave, it was Christmas Eve morning and the task of saying goodbye loomed like a specter before them all. Under the brilliant cold sunlight, tears sparkled on Libby's lashes. "Thank you for everything," she said huskily. She hugged Dixie and Tom. Holt hugged Carrie and Sue and Dixie. Tom even hugged Jill.

"Remember now," called Holt as he swung his daughter into the van and closed the sliding doors. "You're all expected to come to Florida in June as my guests."

"We'll be there," vowed Dixie tearfully. "Goodbye and be careful."

They waved until the house disappeared around a bend in the long drive. Libby relaxed against the seat with a heavy sigh. Jill was quiet in the back seat, and Holt seemed lost in his own thoughts.

The feeling of letdown weighed heavily on Libby. What would happen now? Her car was being towed to Nashville this morning, but the man at the automobile club didn't hold out much hope that it could be repaired until after Christmas. Something had happened to the starter and the mechanics were all away for the holidays. She had two more days at least, depending on the damage, before she could resume her trip.

Holt and Jill had no reason to delay; they could drop her at a hotel in Nashville and be on their way. That thought depressed her even more. Her family, when she'd finally reached them on the telephone, had been generous with commiseration and relieved that she was safe; but there had also been an "I told you so" in her mother's voice.

As Holt merged with the light traffic on the interstate, Libby stared blindly through the window, fighting the urge to cry as uninhibitedly as Jill had. Her hand was engulfed in a warm clasp.

"Hey," said Holt softly. "What's the matter?"

Unable to speak, she shook her head, avoiding his eyes.

"Look at me."

She complied, dredging up a watery smile. "I'm just sad for some reason."

He lifted her hand to his lips, brushing kisses across her knuckles. It was the first time he'd shown any overt affection since the night they'd danced in the parlor. She had begun to wonder if she had dreamed the electric desire that had crackled between them. She had had a lot of eggnog and had been more than a little loose.

Now she was thrilled by the sensation of heat traveling up her arm from his hand. At the same time, the tender gesture added weight to her gloomy mood. In only a short while, they would be separated. She would see them again—she had no doubt about that—but how long would she have to wait and would it be the same between them?

"We'll be there in less than an hour, but then we've got a long day ahead of us." Holt interrupted her thoughts in a low voice.

She didn't understand. "Why? What do we have to do?"

"Well, first we have to check into the hotel."

Libby caught her breath, afraid to speak. Was he actually saying he and Jill were going to stay over?

"And then we have to do some shopping." He threw a look over his shoulder to make sure Jill wasn't listening. "I made arrangements for Santa Claus to come down a certain chimney in Florida, but I'd better have something in Nashville, too, don't you think, if we're going to celebrate Christmas there? Hey!"

Libby had thrown her arms around his neck and was covering his cheek with damp kisses. "Thank you! Oh, Holt, thank you."

"You're going to send us into the ditch again," he protested, laughing. "We should keep one vehicle in working order."

She sat back, unable to keep the broad smile off her face. *I probably look like some grinning idiot.*

Holt took her hand again, raising it to his lips. "Did you think I would leave you alone for Christmas?" he asked softly. "Not a chance."

7

THE HOTEL WAS SO UNDERSTATED that it didn't even have a sign outside. Script letters identified the street name and number.

But the moment she entered, Libby realized this was someplace special. An attendant in a glass-enclosed cubicle had checked their names from a list before releasing the lock to allow them to enter a downstairs foyer.

"Holt, I'm not sure I like the idea of being locked in a hotel."

He grinned and shifted Jill to his other hip so that he could take her hand. They began to mount a wide circular staircase. "Honey, they're not locking you in, they're locking everyone else out. This is where most of the recording stars stay when they're in town to work and need some privacy. And a perfect place for us to spend Christmas. Wait and see."

The lobby was elegant, as much of a contrast to an ordinary hotel as was the method of gaining entrance. There were no lounges or bars, not even a restaurant, in sight. A crystal chandelier bounced prisms of light off mahogany paneling and deep luscious carpeting in a rich shade of red. Holt led the way toward the registration desk.

Libby stopped him, holding out her arms. "Why don't I take Jill while you register, if you have to do such a mundane thing in a place like this."

The truth was she was more than a little intimidated by the silence. What on earth were they going to do with Jill? Though unique and interesting, the hotel didn't seem the type of establishment that would cater to children.

She told Holt so as they entered the elevator. "And what about our luggage?" she added testily over the head of the child who clung to both their hands. Jill had been very subdued since they'd arrived.

Amusement glittered in his eyes. "Music Square Manor caters to any little wish your heart desires." The elevator doors slid silently open, and with a gallant wave he motioned for her to go ahead.

"Is that the name of this place?" she said, as she preceded him. "I would never have known."

"That's it," he assured her happily. "And your luggage will be waiting for you in—" he glanced down at the key in his hand and up at the door in front of them "—here."

"How is it supposed to get here, fly?" she asked as he fitted the key in the lock. "Everything was in the van not less than five minutes...a...go." Her words trailed off as he opened the door and stood back for them to enter.

Jill's delightful laughter rang out. She dropped both their hands and clapped her own at the scene before her. "Look, Daddy. Look, Libby! Look!"

Whatever Libby had expected of the accommodations, it certainly had not been this. The room was at least thirty feet long and almost as wide. One end was furnished as a living room with wonderful chintz-covered upholstered pieces, designed for comfort rather than show, and grouped around a wood-burning fireplace, which was stacked and ready for the touch of a match. The furniture was upholstered in subdued shades of palest peach and rich hunter green, the colors repeated in the draperies and carpeting. Soft strains of Christmas music filled the air. Libby looked around for the source and spied a tape deck on the built-in bookcase beside the mantel.

At the other end of the room, centered under a chandelier, was a dining table with a shining wood finish. Other pieces, a buffet, end tables and coffee tables, added to the illusion that she had just walked into someone's home.

But the center of interest in the marvelous room was a huge sweet-smelling Douglas fir that brushed the ceiling. Multicolored lights and balls, tinsel and old-fashioned strings of popcorn adorned the tree. It wasn't a stylish tree; it looked more like something off a nineteenth-century greeting card. It was absolutely perfect in this room.

Holt pocketed the key and closed the door behind them, watching their reactions with an amused smile. He wrapped his arms about Libby and pulled her back against him. "Like it?" he murmured into her hair.

"It's beautiful," Libby breathed. "Absolutely perfect. I feel as though I've stepped into the privacy of someone's living room."

He left a tender kiss at her neck and released her. "Come on, let's see the rest."

Bedrooms opened at each end of the long room, and true to his word, their luggage was in place, delivered by an unseen hand. "All our meals will be served in the dining area. All we have to do is order, anytime, twenty-four hours a day. If the chef doesn't have what we happen to have a craving for, he'll do everything possible to get it for us."

"You seem very pleased with yourself, Mr. Whitney, but I have to admit you were right."

"Have I ever disappointed you, Miss Hamilton?" He grinned.

Jill ran past them to stake her claim on the bed she wanted. She tugged at the buttons of her coat. "Are you going to sleep in here with me, Libby?"

Libby hesitated, and before she could answer Holt replied for her. "We'll decide who sleeps where later, sweetheart. Now, we need to make some phone calls and then do some Christmas shopping."

He turned to Libby. "I want to call Jill's mother to let her know we're okay, and I'm sure you want to call your parents. Why don't you use the phone in here?"

"Libby, are you ready to go shopping?" Jill called her from the living room a few minutes later. "We're ready."

"Coming," she answered. She frowned at the receiver under her hand. She had just hung up after one of the most unpleasant conversations she'd ever had with her mother. Standing abruptly, she reached for her coat.

Jill had wound her chubby arms around one of her father's legs and was looking up the long distance to his face. "Will we see Santa in the store?"

"Sure," he told his daughter, but his eyes were fixed on Libby. "Okay?" he asked.

She shrugged and nodded, successfully wiping the sadness from her expression. "Fine," she said with an attempt at gaiety. "I'm ready to buy a few Christmas presents. How about you, Jill?"

In the elevator Holt pressed for an answer.

"I got the idea they've washed their hands of their baby," she finally admitted. "Did you complete your call?"

"Jill's mother was at an audition." His mouth twisted wryly. "I talked to an answering machine."

"Can I pick out my own present from you, Daddy?" Jill piped up from between them. "I want a kitten."

"A kitten? You never told me you wanted a pet."

"You never asked me," said his daughter.

JILL WAS FINALLY PERSUADED that the best kittens lived in Florida, and she could have one as soon as they were at home. At the mention of home her face took on the pinched look, but both Libby and Holt set out to distract her, so that in only a few minutes she was laughing again.

The large department store was crowded with frantic shoppers who had waited until the day before Christmas. As Libby, Holt and Jill wandered up and down the aisles, enjoying the bustle and the music, the colors and the smells of Christmas, a voice over the intercom reminded them that the store would close promptly at five o'clock so the employees could get home to their own families, and told them to have a merry holiday.

Holt paused in their ramblings to glance at his watch. "That gives us two hours. Why don't we split up for half an hour and meet somewhere?" His eyes held a twinkle reminiscent of a Christmas elf. The wave of shoppers parted to flow around them.

"Okay. I'll take Jill," said Libby. "Where shall we meet?"

"No, I'll take her with me," Holt replied, a frown building a bridge between his brows as he realized that a certain amount of conspiracy was going to prove necessary if he was to contrive a surprise or two.

Neither of them noticed the frightened confusion on the face of the child linking them with her hands.

A heavy woman with a burden of packages jostled Libby. Smiling vaguely at the woman's distracted apology, she spoke pointedly to Holt. "But you have some private shopping to do, don't you?" she asked, her voice stressing the word 'private.'

"Yes," he yielded. "Well, one of us can take her now; then we'll meet back somewhere and swap."

Holt went down on his haunches in front of the child. "Who do you want to go with first, sweetheart?"

To his astonishment, Jill burst into tears. Responding instinctively and immediately to her distress, Holt scooped her up, holding her close. His broad hand stroked her back in an attempt to assuage her unhappiness, but he felt as though the breath had been knocked out of him.

"What is it, darling?" he murmured. "What's the matter?" The small body in his arms trembled, and he experienced her pain as if it was his own. Would he ever be an adequate father? How did other men do it? He motioned for Libby to join them at the side of the aisle, away from the flow of people.

Libby added her hand to his at Jill's back. "Honey, what's wrong?" The two adults looked helplessly at each other while the child sobbed into his neck. Unerringly her thumb went into her mouth.

"Come on," Holt finally said softly to Libby. "I have an idea."

Trailing along behind him, Libby searched her mind for a reason for Jill's misery. The child had chattered happily over lunch; she had been entranced afterward when they'd stopped in the center of the mall to watch a puppet show. She ran back over their conversation just before Jill had started crying. Oh, no! She couldn't have thought...

She quickened her footsteps to draw alongside Holt. "I think I know what's bothering her," she said quietly.

"Yeah, so do I." He had reached the escalator, and as he spoke he stepped onto a stair.

Libby took the one below them. "She thought we were trying to get rid of her," she told him clearly so the child could hear her. The sobs subsided, and Jill rolled her head sideways on her father's shoulder. She seemed to be listening, but Libby couldn't be sure.

Holt immediately picked up on Libby's intention. "As though we would ever want to be separated from her."

"But she's only a child, Holt. She isn't old enough to understand about surprises." Jill raised her head to look warily at Libby, but Libby pretended to ignore her. "It's a shame, because they're so much fun." She shook her head with mock sadness as she followed Holt off the escalator.

Jill took a shuddering breath. "I do so know about surprises," she said around her thumb.

"Do you?" Libby feigned amazement. Her heart was doing skips as she realized where they were. *Holt, you are a genius.*

Jill nodded. She took her finger out of her mouth. "But sometimes surprises aren't nice," she said soberly, her blue eyes reflecting such hurt that Libby wanted to cry, too.

"At Christmas *all* the surprises are good ones," Libby informed the child positively.

"Like this one," Holt added.

Jill turned to see what her father was talking about. She caught her breath at the sight, and Libby grinned in delight as tears and sadness were completely forgotten.

Santa Claus sat on a golden throne, his crimson-covered belly shaking under the black shiny belt as laughter and happiness rolled magnanimously out of his large chest. This one needed no padding and no fake beard. The full head of white hair was real, too, slightly long and blending almost perfectly with the white fur collar. His dimpled cheeks shone red without the aid of makeup. He was the most beautiful Santa Libby had ever seen.

Dozens of children accompanied by parents formed a line to his left. One child slid off his lap and scampered away to his mother; Santa motioned to the next little boy, who hesitated only briefly before taking his place on the generous knee.

"Would you like to talk to Santa, sweetheart?" Holt asked his daughter gently. "You could tell him what you want for Christmas."

"Could he get me anything I want?"

Holt thought for a minute. "He can't always get you anything you want, but he will try. He is a very loving person, you see. His love for all the children is what makes him so special."

Jill glanced at her father, then back to the enthralling sight before her. "I don't know," she said in a small faltering voice.

"Would you like to stay and watch him for a while?"

Jill nodded, secure in her father's arms as she watched the jolly red-coated figure.

The attraction of Santa soon overcame Jill's misgivings. By the time they reached the front of the line, she was quivering with both anticipation and dread. When the laughing man signaled to her that she was next, she looked to her father for reassurance.

"We'll both be right here," Holt said softly.

Libby held her breath as Jill went toward the man in red. She wore a serious expression, but her footsteps didn't falter.

"Try to hear what she asks for." Holt's hand rested naturally at Libby's waist as he leaned down to speak in a quiet voice. The possessive caress was so natural that he probably didn't even know what he was doing to her, but Libby was instantly aware of the warmth from his fingers. She forced her attention back to the child.

Jill foiled them. Tugging on his beard, she drew Santa's head down and spoke at length and seriously into his ear. His eyes sought Libby and Holt where they stood. He smiled, shrugging helplessly, studied them for a minute and then whispered something back to Jill, which brought a beaming smile to her face. The whispered dialogue went on for several minutes before Santa lifted Jill off his lap and handed her a lollipop. She thanked him and came running over to where they waited.

"Santa's real nice. I'm ready to look for surprises now. Who gets me first?"

"I do," they both said at once.

Jill nodded sagely. "Santa said you'd pro'bly say that." She grabbed her father's hand and tugged. "C'mon, Daddy. Let's go."

Holt's expression and surprised smile brought a lump to Libby's throat.

"We'll meet you back here in an hour, okay?" he called as his daughter dragged him away.

THEY RETURNED TO THE HOTEL a little after five, arms laden with packages. Libby kicked off her shoes as soon as she got inside the door, leaving them where they fell. "Thank goodness! I don't think I could have walked another inch," she said, dropping her packages in a heap and collapsing beside them on the sofa.

"Me, neither," said Jill in a perfect imitation next to her.

"You little devil. Make fun of me, will you?" Libby scooped her up and started to tickle her. Her giggles were happy, the unlucky misunderstanding that had marred her day forgotten now. The conversation with Santa Claus had certainly produced a miracle.

Holt consulted with Libby about their dinner arrangements, then made a call to the service desk. "Our meal will be here at seven. Why don't you rest for a while? Jill and I have some presents to wrap."

"That sounds like a wonderful idea," Libby agreed. She had a few surprises of her own. "Then we'll swap again, shall we?" She winked at Jill.

"Yeah, Libby and I have some things to wrap, too."

She had shopped for small gifts for Holt and Jill, and helped Jill pick out a present for her father, too. She had another thought. "Shall we dress for dinner?"

"Of course," said Holt. "It's Christmas Eve."

"I'll wear my new dress," decided Jill. Libby had bought her a confection of burgundy velvet and off-white lace with matching tights. The child had a streak of femininity a mile wide that Libby had an idea she'd have to fight to maintain, growing up in a house with a man as masculine as Holt.

LIBBY HAD SENT most of her clothes to Florida with her household effects, by moving van. The only cocktail dress she had was a grayish-blue silk chiffon, more suited to warm weather than cold. She gave her hair—shining, squeaky clean and tumbling free over her shoulders—one last swipe with a brush. She fitted carved lapis lazuli leaves in her pierced ears.

A devilish, mischievous smile curved her lightly glossed lips as she faced herself in the mirror. The exaggerated mandarin neckline circled just beneath her chin, the tightly fitted sleeves ending at her wrists. But the fabric was like the fog of an August dawn, sheer and misty over the strapless slip. Her fair skin glowed enticingly through the material.

Her eyes were drawn to another corner of the mirror. She and Jill had wrapped their gifts. They were piled in the middle of the bed, a festive jumble of colors.

A knock on the bedroom door startled Libby out of her reverie. Holt's voice was clear through the polished wood panels. "Libby, dinner will be here in about five minutes."

"Coming." She sprayed on her favorite perfume and walked to the door, the hem of the dress brushing her knees.

Soft music, candles, a centerpiece of red carnations, the spicy-smelling tree that glimmered with multicolored lights, a child sitting on the floor poking curiously at gaily wrapped packages...and a man, smiling gently, contentedly on the scene, caused Libby to halt in the doorframe. She reaffirmed to herself that she wasn't ready for all this domesticity. A romance with a sensual, exciting man, yes, but this scene had all the earmarks of permanence.

"Jill, why don't you get the other packages off the bed?" she asked to break the spell.

"Okay," the child agreed readily. She jumped up.

Holt turned to meet her eyes. He wore a dark-gray suit with a blindingly white shirt and muted red tie knotted under the collar. He looked big, and dangerous, and fabulous. "Hi," he said softly, holding out his hand.

She swallowed a lump in her throat, putting her hand in his. "Hi."

Jill brushed past them, her arms loaded with packages. "I'll put them under the tree."

"Fine. Thank you, darling," Libby murmured distractedly.

Holt leaned forward, inhaling her perfume. "That's nice," he said in a low voice. Using the hand he held, he drew her closer until only inches separated them. "You are a beautiful lady." His eyes sparkled blue arcs as they roamed over her features, lit with flashing glints as they touched her skin, her lashes, taking fire when they reached her lips.

Her eyes fastened on his tie in defense, but she found to her dismay that sight wasn't the only sense that was totally affected by him. The scent of his after-shave, the feel of his slightly roughened palm under her fingertips, the husky echo of his compliment were all as potent as the look of him. "Thank you," she murmured.

She felt his breath on her cheek, the touch of his lips at the corner of her mouth. "More than beautiful," he whispered over her lips. "Exquisite and infinitely desirable."

She inhaled, a long shaky sound of surrender. Her lips parted on his name.

Holt sighed and, checking to see that his daughter was once again engrossed, snaked an arm around her, catching her against his length. "Oh, Libby, I want you," he groaned into her mouth. "These past few days, you'll never know what a hard time I had keeping my hands off you."

His kiss was hungry, insistent, barely restrained. "Tonight." He lifted his head to spear her with his gaze. His demand was also a question.

Libby touched his face, letting the backs of her knuckles brush lightly across his lips. She smiled her answer—there had never really been any doubt, she had just tried to tell herself there was—and then his mouth was back, tasting her, his need a growing hardness against her belly.

Suddenly he was still. If Libby hadn't been so swept up in the glory of his kiss and what it was doing to her, she would have laughed. His tongue traced the line of her lower lip, but absently, his attention diverted to the hand that moved experimentally over the bare skin of her back. "Honey, this dress is indecent," he said after he had explored thoroughly.

"I know," she answered. From waist to neck, from shoulder to shoulder, there was only a bare expanse of skin.

He lifted his head. "You look so…so demure from the front." He seemed hard pressed to understand and was having real difficulty breathing.

"I know," she repeated. "Do you mind?"

"No!" he denied quickly. The exclamation brought them to the attention of the child across the room.

"Libby, come see all the presents!"

Holt released her reluctantly, and she heard him catch his breath as she moved toward the tree and the child; he received the full panoramic impact of the dress. She had never worn it before, and she realized she would have to be very careful where she wore it from now on.

A knock on the door of the suite had Holt looking around in desperation. "Shall I let him in?" he asked dazedly.

"Holt, for heaven's sake, it's just a dress."

"Like the Hope Diamond is just a rock," he growled. "Put yourself on the sofa and don't get up."

To help save his reason Libby complied, sitting with her back pressed firmly against the cushions while the white-jacketed waiter served their table. Jill went over to investigate.

Holt finally handed the man a bill and said, "Thanks, we'll take care of ourselves from here."

"Thank you, sir. Merry Christmas."

Dinner conversation was easier thanks to the fact that Libby sat facing Holt over the length of the table. He could hardly keep his eyes from her, and his stunned expression finally provoked a question from his daughter.

"Are you all right, Daddy?"

"Fine," he answered absently. Libby smiled knowingly.

Jill carried most of the conversation, anyway. Her childish excitement was palpable, bringing smiles to the faces of the two adults. "Libby said she would read me a special story, Daddy. About Santa Claus. What was it, Libby?"

"'A Visit from Saint Nicholas.'"

"That's Santa's other name. Can we get up real early in the morning?" she pleaded.

"As early as you like, Jill," promised her father.

"Not too early, or we might see Santa Claus, and he said we shouldn't see him."

"That reminds me," said Libby. "You and Santa talked a long time. What did he say to you?"

Jill looked from one of them to the other. She furrowed her brow. "I'm not sure I'm sup'osed to tell. I think it's a secret."

"Oh, dear, then I shouldn't have asked. Secrets are like surprises, very special things."

Jill's brow cleared. "I know," she said happily.

After dinner they hung the bright-red knitted stocking Libby had bought that afternoon. Then the three of them sat together before the fire, while Libby read the lovely old poem that began, "'Twas the night before Christmas...'"

Holt held Jill on his lap and Libby under his arm. He was quiet, savoring the atmosphere.

By the time the story was over Jill was yawning, but she insisted on putting out a plate for Santa with a piece of fruitcake provided by the waiter. She was finally convinced to take off the beautiful dress Libby had given her and get into her pajamas.

"Aren't you going to bed, too?" she asked her father. "Santa won't come until everyone's in bed."

"Grown-ups don't go to bed as early as children," he explained. "You know that."

"But if you don't go to bed, it won't hurry up and be morning," she argued with childish reason.

"How do you answer such rationale?" Holt asked Libby with a grin.

She grinned back. "You can't."

He lifted Jill high into the air. "Come on, squirt."

She squealed in delight. "Libby, too," she demanded, and Libby got up to follow. Extra hugs and kisses and glasses of water, and a plea for a night-light used up almost half an hour and a great deal of her father's patience. "Jill," he said in a warning tone when she again appeared at the door to the room she would share with Libby.

"Yes, sir," said Jill in a meek little voice, but she looked pleased and didn't come out again. When Holt went in to check on her a few minutes later, she was sound asleep.

He returned shaking his head. "I don't think I'll ever understand kids," he said. "She seems to enjoy seeing me lose my patience."

"It shows that you care enough to discipline her. Do you remember when she spilled her milk?"

"She cried like crazy."

"Because you didn't fuss, she thought you didn't care."

"That doesn't make sense." He shed his jacket and sank onto the sofa beside Libby. "But I'm not in the mood to reason it out tonight. At last," he sighed, loosening the knot of his tie and unbuttoning the top button of his shirt. "I didn't think I was ever going to get you alone."

Libby watched the typically masculine gesture with a tightening feeling in her abdomen. It was the formal signal of civilized man; the veneer was about to be put away for more earthy pursuits.

Throughout the evening the direction of Holt's thoughts had been easy to chart, she thought as she shied away from staring at him. He'd avoided looking at her for too long a time after Jill's comment during dinner, but his sensual awareness was almost tangible, an essence in the atmosphere, and impossible to ignore.

Libby knew because she was feeling the same impatience to be alone with him, to feel his lips, his hands, to know the weight of his body. Tonight, he had said, and she recognized the candor, the honesty of the words. He wasn't being arrogantly male, he wasn't showing his domination. He was simply stating a fact, and she felt no obligation to argue with him.

What was an appropriate measure of time for lovers to have known each other? Less than a week? Or longer than forever? Duration no longer mattered. The quality of the moments together mattered, not the quantity. Holt had revealed himself to be sensitive and strong. Noble was the rather old-fashioned but appropriate word that came to mind. He would probably wring her neck if she called him noble, she thought with a trace of amusement....

8

LIBBY TURNED HER HEAD against the cushion to find Holt looking at her. His expression was tender and knowing as he held her eyes. Yet he asked, proof that his thoughts paralleled hers. "We are going to make love tonight, aren't we?"

She curled up facing him, her head tilted at an angle, her fingers linked in her lap. Her cheek rubbed lightly, like the caress of a sleek cat, against the back of the sofa. Slowly her mouth curved into a smile of expectancy; her eyes promised. "I don't think I could ever forgive myself if I missed this chance," she said softly, lazily.

His chuckle was deep and smoky as he hooked his arm over her shoulder to pull her into his embrace. He held her, content to look. His hand lay gently at the side of her head, his thumb moving over her temple.

Holt was in no hurry now. The impatience and restless excitement that had driven him through the evening had faded to the sweetness of her acquiescence. He knew those feelings would return as passion built, but for now he wanted to go slowly, savor the texture of her body, the flavor of her skin. He wanted to watch the nuances of her facial expression as he made love to her. He wanted to please her sexually, but more than that, he wanted to inspire a deeper emotion in her, an emotion he was experiencing for the first time in his life. He was no longer afraid to put a name to it.

Deep and awesome, seasoned with physical desire but with a foundation buried in feelings much more enduring, the sensation was foreign to him. He welcomed it willingly, exultantly. It was love.

He had loved Linda with the infatuation of a young man for a beautiful woman. After the infatuation had died, his love had become affection. With the birth of their child, they had both hoped to rekindle those exciting youthful emotions. But true to the quotation, they had put away childish things, both of them. Had the marriage continued, resentment—hers for the trap of marriage, his for her indifference to the vows they had made—would have grown to destructive bitterness.

Eagerly Libby lifted her lips for his first kiss…and the memories of another woman, of any other woman he'd ever known, were swept away in a surge of sensitivity for this one. Dipping his head, he formed his lips over hers gently, tenderly, not a kiss but a taste of her honeyed warmth. However, he had greatly overestimated his own control.

She laid her hand on his chest, and his heart bounded wildly in response. Lowering her lashes, she touched her tongue to his, and he almost exploded. With a sudden movement he lifted her over him and leaned back against the arm of the sofa. Her hair spilled around them, filtering the glow of the lamps to a fine gold radiance. The skin of her bare back was an expanse of satin open to his hands, and he reveled in the feel of her breasts pushing his chest down, down farther into the cushions until he was floating.

While their lips explored, he pushed her hair aside to seek the fastening at her nape. His fingers struggled to find the combination that would free her from the prison of a dress. Clumsy! He who could make love with skill and patience learned many years ago was as clumsy as a damned ox! He moaned his frustration and grabbed her shoulders to lift her up a fraction; he couldn't stand for her to be any farther away. "Honey, how do I get this damned thing off?"

Her eyes were languorous when she lifted her lids to look down at him. "What?" she asked, arousal slurring her speech.

He smiled at her distraction. "The dress. I can't figure out how to get you out of it."

"Oh." She still looked at him, her lips like crushed rose petals, curved into a soft smile.

He groaned aloud. "Libby, darling...please. Help me."

Finally the haze cleared from her eyes, and a becoming blush colored her cheeks. She struggled to sit up.

He groaned again, in pain this time, not passion. Unfortunately she was still on top of him, and her struggles were decidedly uncomfortable until he got her rearranged.

"Sorry," she said with a little smile.

"Witch," he grumbled good-naturedly.

Clumsy! Libby almost cried at her own ineptness. He must think her totally inadequate. She reached for the tiny hooks. Her fingers seemed to all be thumbs, but at last the two sections of the collar parted. She brushed the material aside and lifted her hair to pull the strands free that had caught on a hook.

She glanced at Holt with an apology in her eyes and ready on her tongue. And froze.

Holt's blue gaze was fixed on her breasts, their tips barely covered by the fabric and provocatively tilted by the position of her arms. His eyes were slightly glazed, the skin over his cheekbones flushed, and he seemed to be as bemused as she had been seconds ago. "That's the sexiest sight I've ever seen," he said hoarsely.

A powerful thrill raced through Libby, a measure of sexuality that she'd never been aware of in herself. With a rush of embarrassment, she realized she was playing the unfamiliar role of femme fatale. She quickly lowered her arms, catching the fabric with a hand at her throat.

"Honey, no." Sitting up quickly, he reached out to enfold her in a tender, reassuring embrace, his arms hard and warm around her. "Don't be careful with me. I want all of you. You're a beautifully sensual woman. Don't hide it."

"I'm not hiding," she protested weakly. "I'm just..." *Just what?* she asked herself. *Just confused? Just alive with emotions I've never felt before? Just unable to understand and rationalize those emotions,* she admitted silently. *This is an affair, but I'm more than casually involved. And I'm scared to feel this way, scared to death.*

Holt slid his arm under her knees and stood. A half smile that smacked of too much masculine assurance put her off for a minute as she looped her arms around his neck and looked up into his face. Then she saw the hint of vulnerability in his eyes. He wasn't as confident as she'd first thought. With that discovery, all her doubts were magically washed away. They were a man and a woman, alone within themselves, reaching out to each other, in affection, in need, in desire. Whatever came of tonight, it was right.

She tightened her hold and kissed the strong plane of his jaw, as lightly as a butterfly's wings would brush. In response he lengthened his stride toward the bedroom. He nudged the door closed with his toe until the latch caught. The sound was large in the sudden darkness. Crossing the floor with unerring footsteps, he placed her on the mattress. The bed dipped next to her hip as he sat and reached out a hand to the bedside lamp.

The circle of light had a rosy tint that subdued the prosaic background and blurred the planed, straight edges in the room to soft shadows. This bedroom was exactly like the one she shared with Jill, except in the place of the twin beds there was a king-sized one. Two rooms, so alike and so different, and all because of a bed and a low-wattage, rosy-tinted light bulb.

"You have a very sexy smile on your face," he murmured, leaning forward to brush her jaw with his lips, to luxuriate in her feminine fragrance.

"I'm glad. I want to be sexy for you."

He took hold of her shoulders and she was lifted to within an inch of his face. In the same smooth movement Holt fell back on the mattress, holding her above him, laughing huskily. "This is my ultimate fantasy. I've thought of this moment since I saw you in that truck stop. You're here, in my bed, and I'm not about to let you get away."

She looked around at herself, sprawled on top of him. "I don't seem to be struggling too hard."

He brought her down an inch to give her a quick, hard kiss. "The only thing I need to know right now, honey, is how to get you out of this damned dress."

Libby laughed softly, tracing his intriguing dimple with a forefinger. "Maybe you'll decide it's not worth the effort."

"Not a chance," he said, bringing them both upright once more. "Now, what do we do first?"

She held up her wrist and narrowed her eyes, squinting in the dim light. "There are some little hooks here, but I can't see them in this shadow."

"I'll find them," he vowed gruffly, and set to work.

A stream of soft curses accompanied his struggle, but finally he had her released from the wrist bands. "At last." He started to slide the material off her hands.

"There's another hook around here and a small zipper." She twisted in his arms to show him her back.

He didn't touch her for a minute, and she turned to look over her shoulder. His thundering frown prompted a giggle.

"You find the craziest things to laugh about," he complained. "Whatever diabolical designer dreamed up this dress had a...a cruel sense of humor... All this. . .beautiful skin showing and the rest of you...locked up tighter than a miser's pocketbook."

The giggle grew to full laughter as he mumbled and fumbled until he at last had her free. "Now," he growled triumphantly, tossing the dress aside, "we'll see who has the last laugh." He turned her to face him again.

Suddenly the humor in the situation drifted away on a puff of sensual awareness. Holt's hands closed gently on her shoulders as his gaze traveled over her breasts and down. The lacy, blush-colored bikini panties and garter belt rode low on the gentle swell of her hips. "My Lord!" whispered Holt. "I've heard about these things, but..."

The smile that lingered on Libby's lips softened at the wonder in Holt's eyes. Entranced by his deep-blue gaze, she became elemental woman, reveling in the admiration of her man, strong with the eternal power of her femininity. And generous in her desire to share with him the glorious emotion that even now was blooming, swelling, filling every millimeter of her body with warmth and anticipation.

His hand hovered over her breast, yet she gently stopped its progress, knowing that if he touched her she would go up in flames. "My turn," she said huskily. She reached for the already loosened tie. With a swift tug it was gone. Her fingers were nimble in her haste to open his shirt. The hard musculature of his chest was a magnet to her hands, and she explored the hair-roughened skin, indulging herself in the sensation.

Though he held himself in steely control, Holt couldn't check the gasp that escaped as her fingers brushed his flat nipples. "Honey..." he began in a deep voice.

She lifted her eyes to meet his dark look. "You don't like that?" she asked with a small smile that said she knew very well he liked it.

"I'll get you for this," he said against her lips, and pulled her forward until her nipples were buried in the curling hair of his chest. Slowly he moved her against him. They both cried out with the sensation.

Holt dropped his head to her shoulder as though he no longer had the strength to hold it erect. She could feel the perspiration on his brow. He made a tremendous effort to calm his breathing. "Slow down," he whispered, and then repeated the words over and over.

Libby realized he was speaking not to her but to himself. She lifted her hands to bury them in his hair, comforting him, reassuring him with consoling strokes. "Darling, I don't want you to slow down. Don't treat me as though I were glass, Holt."

She didn't know what she was offering. With a superhuman effort he brought his raging desire under control, his control a tenuous thing. Firmly he urged her backward on the bed. His fingers only trembled slightly as he unhooked the gossamer hose and peeled them from her long legs. The lacy garter belt came next. He tried to focus on the tiny pink rose just below her navel rather than the enticing shadow beneath the matching undergarment, but when she lifted her hips to help him in his task, he squeezed his eyes shut for a breathtaking moment.

Finally the last barrier was removed. He stood and stripped his own clothes off in almost one motion. Then and only then did he allow himself the luxury of a complete inventory of the exquisite creature before him. Her skin was warm ivory tinted with rose. The golden mane spread across the pillow, gleaming in the soft light from the lamp. One leg was bent slightly in an enticing pose as old as Eve.

When he lowered himself to the bed beside her, he was almost overcome by her fragrance...a bouquet of wildflowers and musk and fresh femininity. His own voice sounded strange to his ears as he spoke. "You are so sweet...so absolutely, lusciously sweet." He dipped his head to take in a long, deep breath, savoring the scent of her hair. "You smell sweet."

Libby closed her eyes in anticipation of his touch as his hand lingered in the air above her breast for a moment before closing gently over the curve. Instinctively she arched her back, thrusting herself into his hand.

"You feel wonderful...." He continued his verbal seduction while his hand began a tender massage. "So soft and warm and firm. Your skin is like the skin of a peach, smooth and perfect."

He levered himself up until his lips hovered above the crest of the mound he cupped in his broad hand. His tongue flicked out to bathe her nipple.

Libby sucked in her breath. "Holt!" He was driving her wild. She wanted to feel his weight. Her nails scored his shoulder as she urged him down but still he resisted.

"You taste so sweet. Oh, honey, you taste delicious." His mouth opened completely over her, sucking hungrily.

"Please," she whispered. "Now, please."

The constraint he had placed on himself surrendered to her entreaty. Suddenly his hands became restless, moving over her as though they had a mind of their own, moving spontaneously to the places that would be aroused. His lips followed, licking, nibbling, tasting, returning often to cover her own with deep hungry kisses.

Her hands were buried in his hair, sliding over his shoulders, down his back to his lean hips, guiding him with the movement of her body, her soft moans, to her pleasure points, and seeking his.

When his fingers dipped into the warm moist center of her desire, Libby's hips thrust forward and she called his name. Her head dug into the pillow, thrashing from side to side with the ecstasy he ignited. Her arms circled his torso, demanding that he fill this emptiness in her.

His hands tangled in her hair, he paused on the threshold to look down into her eyes, glazed with demand and desire. Sliding slowly, he entered her. She inhaled deeply and let the breath out on a long, long sigh. Their gazes met in mutual gratification and relief. The preliminaries, delightful though they had been, were over. At last they were joined as man and woman were destined to be joined. Her face was wreathed in a beatific smile as she wound her arms around his neck. "It's..." She let her eyes drift blissfully shut.

"Perfect," he finished for her, his voice husky with some profound emotion. "The most perfect thing that's ever happened to me." The last words faded to a whisper as he began to move, in easy strokes at first, letting her accept the feel of him at her own pace. She joined the rhythm, panting now, tiny gasps escaping her desire-reddened lips.

Reflexes took over, intuition that built a passion in him to the point of bursting....

His patience held until he heard her cry of completion, felt her body quake and shudder beneath him, her nails dig into his back, her small white teeth at his shoulder. And then he exploded within her, his entire being lost in world-shaking convulsions. "Ah—Libby," he gasped jerkily. "My beautiful Libby."

Libby fought to regain her breath, but when he would have moved aside, she held him to her. "Stay," she murmured.

"I'm too heavy, honey."

"No."

Cupping her bottom, he rolled to the side, taking her with him, covering her lips with a tender kiss. She lay half sprawled on top of him, her gleaming hair like a blanket over his shoulders, his chest. He stroked its silky length, his fingers weaving among the loose curls, lifting them to catch the light.

He wondered at the feelings that washed over him, feelings of love such as he'd never experienced. He was enthralled with the desirability of this woman, but he wanted her for the rest of their lives, wanted to share everything with her, his laughter and his tears, his love, his strengths and weaknesses, everything life had to offer, everything she went through. Even the sad times would be tolerable if they supported each other.

Holt was surprised at the idea that he could very easily come to depend on her. So much for wanting to take care of her, he thought ruefully. But he wanted to do that, too. He wanted everything. He wanted marriage.

What would she say if he told her he wanted to marry her? She would probably think he was crazy. They had known each other such a short time. Yet his feelings were definitely permanent, cast in concrete, not marred by even a shred of doubt. He loved Libby Hamilton, and he needed her for his wife.

Holt smiled across the top of her head. Jill adored her. Besides, there would surely be other children, beautiful little girls, maybe a son. His arms tightened around her in a hug of anticipation.

Libby had been floating on a cloud somewhere between wakefulness and sleep. She tilted her head back to look up at him. "Why do you have that smile on your face?" she asked drowsily.

He grinned and smoothed away a strand of hair from a corner of her mouth. "What kind of smile?"

"The same kind the cat wore while he licked the feathers off his lips."

Holt laughed. "Because I'm happy, I guess." He couldn't tell her he loved her...ask her to marry him, now. He'd wait. They had a couple of days left in Nashville, depending on how long it took to repair her car—he wasn't going to leave without her—and a day or two more on the road. At least four more days together in such proximity, after which she might be ready for a declaration. They probably knew each other better now than most couples did who had been dating for months, but he'd give her as much time as possible.

Despite her reservations she had to sense the power of this, had to share these feelings. They were strong, unexpected, but no less potent.

"I'm happy, too." Libby curled her body back against him, tucking her head under his chin. She yawned, shifted her leg, running her toes down his calf to fit them into the arch of his foot.

"Libby, will you marry me?" Damn! He *was* crazy!

"What?" She yawned again.

"I said, let's get married." He held his breath.

"That would be nice," she said dreamily.

Abruptly she found herself flat on her back, Holt looming over her with a flame burning in his eyes. "Darling," he breathed, "I know it's quick, but I..." He cradled her cheeks in his hands and covered her lips in a kiss that was like a vow. "I'll make you happy, I promise."

"Are you serious?" She was fully awake now. She held him off with a hand at his chest. "Wait a minute. Holt, I...I thought you were teasing."

He drew back to look at her; a wary, defensive expression dimmed the light in his eyes. "I've never been more serious."

"But we can't...I can't."

Holt berated himself for being such a precipitate fool. She couldn't be expected to feel this gut-wrenching, overwhelming need that had gripped him almost from the moment he'd first seen her. He knew how she felt. Any fool could have predicted her reaction. Ah, hell.

He wouldn't beg, but he would try to explain. "Libby, I want you to know this is the first time I've ever proposed to a woman."

That surprised her. "But...you've been married!"

"Linda and I married because she thought she was pregnant. Something along the lines of, 'You've got to marry me.' A false alarm as it turned out, and I was not unwilling. But I never asked her." His expression was grim now.

"Holt, we need to talk about this. I was half-asleep." Libby sat up, pushing the heavy mane of hair away from her face. Marry him? Her feelings were profound, as she'd just found out, but she wanted time, time to discover and enjoy her freedom. She put her fingers to her temples and pressed hard. "I can't say yes, not now," she whispered.

"You just did," he said bluntly. "What if I said I intend to hold you to it?"

He was pressuring her, and she responded with the resistance that was as much a part of her makeup as her smile. It was a built-in reaction, born and nurtured through the years as a defense against her family, reinforced by the debacle of her engagement. "You're not being fair. I told you. I was half-asleep. You're not going to pressure me into something this important. If I should ever decide to marry, it will be a decision made rationally. Not after a session of lovemaking, when my defenses are down."

"Do you feel you have to be defensive with me?" he asked in a dangerously low voice.

"No. Yes." She spread her hands. "I don't know." Her arms came around to hug her stomach. "I suppose I do."

The body language said it all to Holt. The protective gesture chilled his heart. Who did she think she had to protect herself from? "After what we just shared, that's a hell of a thing to say."

"Then don't push me."

He sighed heavily and withdrew from the argument. He had made a mistake. He would do what he had to, to rectify it. "Look, Libby. I didn't mean to spring this on you so soon. I meant to wait until we both had more time to be sure, but somehow it slipped out. Forget I asked."

Slipped out? Well, that was certainly a casual way to propose to someone. Was he already regretting his impulsive offer? Maybe he thought he'd been too hasty. Libby was not a vacillating, changeable female but, conversely, the withdrawal of his proposal irritated her more than the pressure she had felt from him a moment ago. "Can't you make up your mind?" she demanded sarcastically, the words out before she realized she was going to say them. She pulled the sheet up to hide her breasts.

Holt's jaw went slack with astonishment. "Will you listen to yourself?" he said finally. "Lady, there's someone in this room who can't make up her mind, but it sure as hell isn't me."

Libby sniffed. "I'm going to bed," she announced. She rose and snatched up her dress to drape it around her naked body.

Holt seized her wrist. "You're not going to sleep here...with me?" he grated. He wouldn't beg, dammit! He had only done that once in his lifetime, for the sake of his child, to save a marriage that had been dead for years, and he would never do it again. He was surprised at how much her refusal hurt him. Even though he knew he'd botched it, even though he hadn't given her the time she needed to learn to trust him, he still hurt like hell. He schooled his face to hide his emotions.

Libby looked down at him. The sheet barely covered the lower half of his body, leaving his broad, tanned chest bare. His hair was mussed and shining and too much of a temptation to her fingers. She wanted nothing so much as to crawl back under the sheet with him. It angered her to feel that way.

"No." The one-word answer was cruel, she knew with regret, but he was pushing her again. Right now, all she could think of was getting out of this room, gaining time to put her feelings into perspective. She twisted her wrist in his grasp.

Immediately Holt released her. "Suit yourself," he said, and fell back against the pillows, hooking his fingers together under his head in a determinedly easy pose.

Not until she was safely out of the room, not until the sound of the door closing gently behind her released him, did he allow his fists to clench violently in the sheet or the pain in his expression to show, or the soft curses to escape his lips. *You're a stupid fool*, he berated himself harshly. He knew she was running from family, from commitment, from being tied with loving bonds of any kind. Wasn't he smart enough to plant a seed, nurture it, let it grow to full maturity before he harvested? Instead he had ripped it up before it even had a chance to sprout.

HOLT GLANCED OVER at the bed closest to the window. His daughter was sleeping soundly.

Libby lay curled on her side in the darkened room. Silently he approached the bed and came down on one knee beside her face. She slept with one fist tucked beneath her cheek, the other hand spread beside her on the pillow. Her lips were slightly parted, and her breath feathered a strand of hair that had fallen over her face. Carefully he reached out to lift it away. She sighed restlessly in her sleep. Her tongue came out to moisten her lips.

He leaned forward to touch his lips to her shoulder. Her skin was cool and smooth. His mouth roamed softly across to the slender strap of her gown. He drew back to look at her again as he slipped a finger under the strip of silk and slid it off her shoulder.

A sound escaped her lips, something between a moan and a sigh, but she didn't waken.

Her ear was a delicate shell that he couldn't resist. He leaned forward, blowing gently into it, kissing the soft spot behind her lobe. Then he withdrew again to watch the effects of his tender assault.

She smiled in her sleep. Her lashes fluttered, settled back on her cheeks. She shifted slightly, and he inhaled sharply. Her movement had freed one breast from the bodice of her gown, but she remained on her side, so that the cleavage formed by her position was seductive and totally captivating. In the faint light from the living room, he could see that the cool air was having its effect on her nipple, tightening the rosebud. He wanted to bury his face in the loveliness, feast on her beauty. They had made love only three hours ago, yet he wanted her with the strength of months of frustration.

With a long finger he traced a line from the curve of her shoulder to the swell of her breast. He noted with surprise that his hand was shaking as he drew a circle around the enticing nipple.

He was so enthralled by his action that he failed to realize Libby was awake. Her eyes were large smoky saucers as she watched him. He had on a dark terry-cloth robe and his hair was damp. He smelled of soap, a sharp, bracing smell that was at odds with his expression. Shadows couldn't disguise the lazy desire and hunger there. His touch was feather light, but so effective.... "Holt," she whispered.

His eyes met hers with no attempt to hide his vulnerability. "Let's not fight," he murmured immediately.

She raised her hand to lay it at the side of his face. He had showered but he hadn't shaved. The stubble of his beard was pleasantly abrasive to her palm. "What time is it?"

"About three," he muttered huskily. He kissed her lips lightly. "Truce?"

"Truce," she agreed. "I don't want to fight, either."

"Good." And he whipped off the covers and picked her up in his arms.

"Can we just lie here and talk for a while?" she asked when they were in his big bed once more.

"Can we talk without arguing again?" he countered.

"I don't know, but it's important to me."

He sighed, pulling her back against his chest, his arms a warm haven around her. "Okay, honey. If it's important to you I'll listen."

"When I decided to leave Chicago, it wasn't just a spontaneous decision; it was a giant step. And it cost me." Her voice was a whisper that he had to strain to hear.

"I went through scenes, tears, threats and whatever other forms of torture my family could dream up. I don't think they will ever know what they put me through, because to them it was all done in the name of love."

She turned to look up at him through the shadows. "Please try to understand. I have a new job to settle into. I love my career."

Holt felt a large hand squeeze around his heart, but he kept his features expressionless.

"And it's important, too, for you to spend time with Jill right now." She tried to laugh, but the sound was hollow to her ears. "Very likely you're proposing because you don't know much about children. When you get used to being a father, you'll probably decide you didn't really need me, after all."

He rolled onto his back. She propped up on her elbow to look at the strong, rugged profile. "And maybe you're not telling the whole truth," he said, unable to hide the bitterness in his tone. "Maybe you don't want to be saddled with a child. My ex-wife felt the same way."

Libby kept a leash on her temper. She had just refused the only proposal of marriage this man had ever offered. And it hadn't been offered lightly. Though their brief time together might indicate otherwise, she knew that. She would imagine there were many women who would kill for what she'd thrown away.

"Libby, I'm not trying to take your career away from you," he said by way of apology.

"I know...and maybe things will work out for us." She laid her cheek against his heart. "Just don't mention marriage to me, Holt, please. Not for a long, long time."

"Not for a long time," he agreed.

If their lovemaking held a trace of desperation, both of them pretended not to notice.

9

"HOLT, WAKE UP."

"Hmph."

He slept on his stomach, one arm across her middle in a hold that any wrestler would admire. Libby shook his shoulder. "Wake up, Holt."

He shuddered, flexed his large body and rolled to his side, scooping her closer. "Why? It's still dark outside."

She chuckled. "How do you know? You haven't opened your eyes yet."

"My interior clock tells me so." He nuzzled her neck.

"Well, your interior clock is right, but we have to get up and play Santa Claus."

He opened one eye halfway. "How do we do that?"

"Don't you remember when you were little? You woke up on Christmas morning and went into the living room and saw that *someone* had been there while you slept? Someone had eaten the cake, filled the stockings, left presents?"

Holt opened both eyes to study her. Her eyes were sparkling silver, like the lining of a cloud in a summer sky. No, he didn't remember those things, because they'd never been done for him. "My folks thought believing in things like the tooth fairy and Santa Claus was unhealthy." His tone was noncommittal. "We always just put the presents under the tree."

Libby simply stared at him, not knowing what to say. Her denial of his proposal took on more significance. If anyone needed a complete family this man did. The thought shook her, and she looked away in confusion. What should she say to him?

Suddenly she thought about Jill. It wasn't her place to interfere with the way he reared his child, but the years of childhood wonder were short. Realism would teach its lessons all too soon. Was it harmful to indulge a child in fantasies for those brief years? "You let Jill talk to Santa yesterday," she reminded him softly. Surely he wouldn't be so heartless as to let Jill observe the legend and then tell her there was nothing to it.

Holt slid his fingers into her hair and turned her to face him. "Honey, I'm not trying to say Jill shouldn't believe in Santa Claus," he said gently. "I'm just saying I need you to show me how things like this are done."

Her smile could have lit a dozen trees, Holt thought. He loved her so much, needed her warmth in his life. His parents hadn't been hard people, or unloving, but their affections had been kept deep inside, cloaked in restraint. Libby could do for both him and Jill what, in the early days of his marriage, he had hoped Linda would do—provide some openhanded affection, freely given in the name of love. It was the kind of love he had always dreamed of, warm and tender and giving, spiced with touching and hugging, shorn up by laughter, seasoned with faith and assurance. It was the kind of love he was determined his child would have.

"Come on, then. Let's get started." She threw back the covers and tugged at his hand. "We have to be quiet. It's after six, she'll be up soon."

He came off the bed beside her. "Jill? Uh-uh. She's a late sleeper. She never wakes before eight." Playfully he tried to grab her. "We have plenty of time. Let's go back to bed."

Libby evaded his arms, slipped her gown over her head and emerged, grinning. "Would you like to wager on that? I promise you we don't have time for hanky-panky."

"Who said anything about hanky-panky? I'm sleepy," he complained. A brow waggled suggestively. "You kept me up too late."

She groaned at the double entendre. "Scrooge!" She tossed his robe to him and belted herself into her own.

Thirty minutes later Libby sat beside Holt on the sofa, sipping coffee. She looked around the living room, pleased with what they had accomplished. Holt had replenished the fire in the grate. Its glow and the lights of the tree were the only illumination in the room. A bright-red stocking hung from the mantel. Tangerines and nuts were bulky in the toe, while the knitted cuff at the top bulged with candy canes and a toy flute. Under the tree a sweet-faced baby doll slept in a hand-carved cradle—a surprise from Libby. Holt's choice, a beginner's computer, was assembled and ready for the action games he'd picked to go with it.

Libby turned to smile at him. *This is nice*, she thought. If they were a family, there would be many moments like this, moments of being together in the soft quiet of dawn with a child—or two—sleeping in the next room. She took a slow breath, surprised to find the claustrophobic feeling wasn't as strong as before, when he'd asked her to marry him. *It's the atmosphere*, she told herself. *Christmas is the loving season*. The closed-in sensation would return. Meanwhile she wanted to enjoy the intimacy.

"Would you like to open your presents now before Jill wakes up?" she asked, getting to her feet.

"Isn't that cheating?" asked Holt with a grin.

"Well, maybe just a little." She grinned back, scrambling around among the gaily enclosed gifts until she found two she had wrapped yesterday.

Holt joined her and picked up the one he'd wrapped. They returned to the sofa. Libby's eyes sparkled like a child's.

"You first," he said, placing the box in her hand and taking the two she held out.

Her fingers shook slightly as she tore into the paper. A velvet box was revealed, indicating jewelry of some kind. Her eyes met Holt's in dismay. He wouldn't, would he? She lifted the lid and bit back a gasp. On a bed of white satin rested a delicate golden snowflake suspended from a chain of the same metal. More than an inch in diameter, on each of its six points was set a small diamond. "It's beautiful," she managed. "But, Holt—"

"If you say I shouldn't have, I'll throttle you."

She searched his face. He seemed to be waiting as uneasily as she. She knew from experience how it felt for the recipient of a gift to demur, making the giver seem foolish. The necklace was much too expensive, but she could give him the pleasure of accepting. "I'll have to leave it to Jill in my will to salve my conscience, but thank you," she said sincerely. "Will you help me put it on?" She lifted the chain from the box.

Holt's hands were unsteady at her nape, but finally he fitted the tiny ring to the clasp. He pressed his lips to the spot, sending shivers down her spine. "Merry Christmas," he murmured, pulling her back in his arms for a warm hug.

"Your turn," said Libby huskily, handing him the two packages from her lap. She had found a bestseller Holt had mentioned wanting to read. He was enthusiastic about that. And in the second package there was a soft wool sweater that exactly matched his eyes. She was rewarded with a deep hungry kiss.

"Thank you, honey," he murmured against her lips. "For more than the book and sweater. The gift you gave me last night was the most precious."

Libby succumbed to the temptation of his embrace and melted into him. "For me, too, Holt. I...it was the most wonderful gift I've ever received."

He drew back to look down at her.

Libby dropped her gaze from the intensity of his. She disentangled herself from his arms and laughed in an attempt to lighten the atmosphere. "You make pretty good coffee," she said brightly, reaching for her cup.

"Thanks," he grumbled, curving his arm out to bring her back into a loose embrace and place a kiss on top of her head. "We could have stayed in bed for another hour. I told you Jill's a late sleeper."

"But isn't this beautiful, the tree, the music?"

Holt's gaze followed hers around the scene. "It's very beautiful," he agreed in a low voice.

Snow fell silently beyond the windows, and a tape filled the air with muted strains of "Silent Night." The moment was quiet and peaceful, a time of sharing with no need for conversation. The last notes of the famous carol faded, to be followed by a livelier "God Rest Ye, Merry Gentlemen."

"Daddy, Libby isn't in her bed," came a sleepy voice from the door behind them.

Libby raised up, stopping on the way to give Holt an "I told you so" smile. "Here I am, sweetheart. Come and see what Santa has brought you."

Jill approached the back of the sofa slowly, her thumb in her mouth, dragging the once-pink blanket. The wonder in her eyes grew as she took in the scene. They both turned to watch as she stood on tiptoe to peer between their shoulders.

"Don't you want to come around here so you can see better?" asked Libby softly.

Jill nodded, but she didn't move. Holt reached across the back of the sofa and scooped her up in one arm. He held her securely on his lap for a minute. She looked up at him, in awe of the miracle that had taken place in the room since last night. He felt a strange burning sensation in the back of his throat. Seeing the wondrous display through his daughter's eyes was an experience that touched him deeply.

Finally Jill was ready. She wiggled free, and her chubby little legs carried her in a trot to where the doll and the computer waited.

Libby held her breath. She and Holt had wrangled amiably over which gift would be the first to catch Jill's attention. The child headed straight for the computer. Libby groaned, and Holt laughed.

"So much for chauvinism," he teased as he joined his daughter on the floor. "Come on down here and help. You're the expert."

An hour later Libby was curled up contentedly in one corner of the sofa, her head pillowed on the arm, to watch father and daughter argue good-naturedly over who would play the next game. She smiled to herself. The two heads, one dark and one golden, were tilted toward each other. None of the horrid resignation and reserve that had marred their relationship in the beginning was evident now. Jill's constant chatter was occasionally interrupted by the deep roll of her father's voice. When Libby felt her lids begin to droop, she blinked determinedly to keep them open. Holt wouldn't be pleased if she fell asleep, after waking him so early this morning.

Jill left his side to investigate the doll and cradle and the contents of the stocking, but she kept coming back to the computer. She was a bright child and, with Libby's help, had mastered the basic program in a short time. Then her independent streak took over; she demanded to play alone.

Holt left his daughter engrossed in her game and returned to the sofa to stand over Libby, looking down at her in silence.

Libby rolled to her back, her eyes climbing the length of him. By the time her gaze reached his face, her mouth was dry.

His mind must have been following her thoughts, because his eyes were as dark as midnight when he came down on his haunches beside her. He leaned forward to brush her lips with his own. "If you don't want to be ravished before breakfast, you'd better not look at me like that," he warned in an undertone.

Her smile slowly spread to her eyes. "Ravished before breakfast. That has such a marvelously decadent sound." She yawned, extending her arms over her head in a long, sleepy stretch.

"Libby, have a heart," pleaded Holt, his eyes riveted on the thrust of her breasts against her robe.

She grinned and sat up. "Yes, sir."

He gave her his hand and hauled her to her feet. They joined Jill on the floor beside the tree, where he distributed the remaining gifts.

Holt had insisted on bringing up the presents that Libby's family had put in her car when she'd left Chicago, so she had a mountain to open.

Jill abandoned the computer long enough to help. She and Libby had also picked out a red suede vest for her father. "It's your Santa Claus vest," she proclaimed proudly when he opened the package.

"I'll wear it today," promised Holt.

"Gosh, Libby, you have lots of presents," Jill observed as she tore into a silver-wrapped package.

"I have a big family," Libby explained. The box contained a beautiful gray sweater with a cowl neck from her oldest brother.

"Don't you get anything from Santa?" asked Jill.

"Santa only brings things to children in a family," Libby answered.

"I wish I had a big family," said the child mournfully, reaching for another package. "If you— Oh, no!"

She dropped the gift and clapped her hand over her mouth.

"What is it, Jill?" asked her father.

"Nothing." The child shook her head vigorously. "Santa said you shouldn't tell all your wishes."

Holt looked at Libby, a question in his eyes. She shrugged. The arrival of their breakfast postponed any further probing.

THE STREETS OF DOWNTOWN NASHVILLE were almost deserted and covered with snow when the threesome ventured out after breakfast. The wind still made its chill felt, but bright sunlight warmed their faces. They found a small chapel nearby that was having a Christmas service. For an hour they were stirred by the message and the clear, ringing voices of the choir.

On their way back to the hotel they stopped to build a snowman on the corner. Jill wanted to leave him her hat. Libby couldn't resist stuffing just a *little* snow down Holt's collar, and a vigorous snowball fight ensued.

For Christmas dinner they stuffed themselves on turkey and dressing, candied yams and vegetables, hot rolls and butter, mincemeat pie and coconut cake. They all groaned and collapsed on the king-size bed for a nap while the unobtrusive waiter cleared the table.

Later that afternoon they ordered movies from the extensive library provided by the hotel for the video recorders in each room. They watched *Miracle On Thirty-Fourth Street* and *Rudolph, The Red-Nosed Reindeer.*

Jill spoke for Holt and Libby, too, when she said her prayers that night. "Thank you, God, for the most wonderful day I've ever had."

10

NERVOUSLY LIBBY LOOKED one last time at her car, now repaired. It was hooked on to the rear of the van with a complicated bar arrangement and bearing a sign across the back bumper, Car In Tow.

Once Jill had climbed inside, Holt slid the loading door shut and secured the lock. He stood by the passenger door, holding it open for Libby. The wind ruffled his dark hair, molding the fabric of his plaid shirt to his broad chest. He had tossed the sheepskin jacket into the back of the van. "Let's get going, honey. It's cold."

"Are you sure the car won't come loose?" Libby asked as she put one foot up on the high step. She had visions of her new car breaking free to careen wildly across the interstate.

Holt assisted her with a boosting hand on her fanny. "Positive," he assured her. He slammed the door and circled in front of the van to climb into the driver's side.

Libby twisted in her seat to check on Jill. The child had arranged herself on the long bench with her Christmas treasures on either side of her. Swiveling his seat, Holt turned on the small television. "You'll have to let it warm up for a minute," he told his daughter.

"Do you want to watch TV with me, Libby? We can find some cartoons."

Libby grinned at Holt, who grinned back and gave her knee a squeeze before starting the engine. "Thanks, Jill. I think I'll stay up here and help your daddy navigate."

Jill's brows met in the middle of a frown. "What's 'navigate'?"

"I need her to help me watch for signs telling me where to go," her father explained as he put the van in gear and eased into the sparse traffic.

"Why?" said Jill.

"So we won't get lost."

"Why?"

"Because we want to go home."

Jill opened her mouth again, but before she could get the word out, Holt gave her a hard look in the mirror. "Jill," he said in a warning tone.

"I forgot," she told him sheepishly, and settled back to watch the animated antics of the characters on the screen.

The interstate took them quickly out of the city into the countryside. The mountains of Kentucky and northern Tennessee had mellowed to rolling hills and miles of pasture land. Though the day was cold and blustery, the sun shone brightly, reflecting an almost blinding whiteness from the snow. "The world looks so clean and unsullied when it's covered with snow, doesn't it?" Libby observed idly.

Holt reached over to take her hand. Linking their fingers, he lifted it to his lips. "And promising. I don't know when I've felt so happy, Libby," he said quietly.

His gaze flicked to her face before returning to the road. "Are you happy, too?"

She smiled, then paused to think. Yes, she supposed so. The only tension that had marred this morning had been the last phone call to her parents, telling them she was ready to leave Nashville. Their voices had been strained and full of reserve. She felt guilty about causing them concern, promising herself that if she ever had children, she wouldn't repeat her parents' mistakes, wouldn't try to bind them to her with guilt.

But her parents were hundreds of miles away, and she was no longer a child. Suddenly she realized that freedom to choose was a strong booster to happiness. She *was* happy, she realized, and told Holt so.

"I like your sweater. Who gave you that?"

"The tag said, 'Larry,' my oldest brother, but Larry's never been shopping in his life. His wife picked it out."

"She has good taste."

"Impeccable taste. Malvina is a buyer for Marshall Field's."

"The phone call this morning upset you, didn't it?" He released her to grasp the steering wheel with both his hands.

"I think they've washed their hands of me," she said wryly.

"I doubt that. You can't turn love on and off like a spigot. You've described them collectively but not individually. Tell me about Larry and Malvina."

Libby watched the long fingers curl around the leather-covered wheel and thought of their touch—so strong, so capable and yet exquisitely gentle. She forced her attention to the scenery beyond the window and began to talk, telling him about the various members of her large family, describing the characteristics that made them individuals and the singular traits that made them alike.

Holt seldom took his eyes from the road, but even when he wasn't looking at her, her image was imprinted on his brain. He loved to watch her. When she smiled he was warmed by her beauty and enthusiasm. Her face was so open, so appealing. Passion would return in the dark hours of tonight, but for now he was content just to be with her, to listen to the music in her voice, to bask in the miracle of her nearness. He was in love with Libby Hamilton, and he loved her. Each day, each hour they spent together reinforced his love. He just wasn't sure how to convince her that they belonged together.

Her reaction when he had mentioned marriage on Christmas Eve was branded on his memory. If they could only discuss the possibility in the light of day, he could convince her that time had nothing to do with his feelings. He might have known her for years. And he had no intention of tying her to home and hearth. She was stubborn and though he was frustrated by her refusal, there was a positive aspect. Over the two days since his ill-fated proposal, he'd learned more about this woman. He had figured out that Libby, in contrast to Linda, loved her career but wasn't obsessed by it.

Holt was obliged to concentrate on his driving as the road began to climb and turn toward Monteagle Mountain. Billboards proclaimed it the highest point between Chicago and Miami. "Downhill all the way from here," he told Libby.

"How much farther, Daddy?" Jill asked from the back seat.

"Don't ask. We still have a long way to go."

"Will we get there this year?"

Libby laughed.

"Barely," said her father.

An hour later Libby spied another billboard announcing that the Chattanooga Choo-Choo was only blocks from Highway I-24 and offered train rides and good Southern cooking as well as lodging. She leaned across the space that separated their seats, whispering so Jill wouldn't overhear. "Why don't we stop there for lunch? It looks like fun."

"What looks like fun?" Jill piped up, over the sound of cartoons.

"Her hearing is sharp." Holt laughed.

"'Acute' is a better word. Shall I tell her?"

"Tell me what?" Jill spoke from between them.

"We're going to stop for lunch at an old train station," Libby explained.

"I have a picture of a train in my book." Jill scrambled back to look through a box of toys and books. "Here it is," she said, holding the book up. She came back to climb onto Libby's lap. "I'll find the page, and you can read it to me."

Her father had another suggestion as he pulled the van into the right lane. "We're almost there. Why don't you look out for the sign with a picture of the train."

"I thought Libby was the na...navigate person."

"Well, she might need some help on this one."

"Okay."

Minutes later they turned into the parking lot of the huge old Union Station Building. "Brrr," said Libby as she shrugged into her coat. "I thought the farther south we were the warmer it would be, but it seems to be getting colder."

Holt paused to look up to the sky with a worried frown before returning his attention to Jill's hooded jacket. "Yeah, it does. Remind me to call home when we stop tonight. I'd better check the Florida forecast." He put on his coat and turned the collar up. "Come on, squirt. Let's get you inside," he said, swinging his daughter up into his arms.

Libby followed his long-legged stride through wrought-iron gates to the neatly trimmed gardens that had replaced most of the former railroad yards. The wind swept across the wide expanse, effectively cutting off any desire to linger and explore. The large doors of the restored railroad station closed behind them with a whoosh.

"How long will it take to reach Macon from here?" Libby asked Holt when they were settled at a table beside a window looking over the gardens. Holt had called ahead for reservations to a hotel in the middle Georgia city.

He looked at his watch. "About four and a half to five hours, depending on the traffic through Atlanta."

"Can we ride on that train, Daddy?" Jill pointed to a steam engine that had pulled to a stop just beyond the window. A group of laughing tourists emerged from the car behind the engine, assisted by a man in an old-fashioned conductor's uniform. Coats were quickly buttoned and collars turned up against the cold as the group hurried to the shelter of the building.

Holt's eyes followed the direction of Jill's finger. "Sure. As soon as we finish lunch. There's supposed to be a model-train museum somewhere in the complex, too."

An hour later, having explored for as long as Holt would allow, they were once again southward bound on Interstate 75. The ribbon of highway wound through the gray-green mountains of northern Georgia and climbed the plateau where Atlanta sat like a jewel in an evergreen crown. The city sprawled in every direction, the massive building projects evidence of its growth into the queen city of the South. Today, however, the queen was bedraggled, shrouded in a foggy mist, her pristine skirts ragged with highway construction and snarled with traffic. When the van finally evaded the last semitrailer truck to exit the perimeter highway and return to Interstate 75, Holt breathed a sigh of relief.

So did Libby. She had moved to the back seat and had spent the past hour trying to keep Jill entertained and quiet. The child's constant questions were being answered by her father with shorter and shorter explanations as the weather grew worse. Libby couldn't blame him for his irritation. The traffic was a nightmare.

They were still inside the Atlanta city limits when the tire blew. Libby, still in the rear seat with Jill, clutched her close as the vehicle lurched.

Holt erupted with a string of curses that colored the air blue as he fought to keep the van under control. He did a superb job, slowing gradually until they could limp to the side of the road.

"What is it, Daddy? What's the matter? Is our van broke?"

Libby, seeing the stiff set of Holt's shoulders, tried to shush the child. A saint's patience would be sorely tried under the circumstances.

Once again Holt surprised her. He heaved a sigh and turned to give them both a rueful grin. "We have a flat tire, squirt. I can fix it, though, so don't be afraid."

The thumb went into Jill's mouth.

"The two of you get on your coats."

"Why?" Jill asked.

"Because it's dangerous for you to sit in a vehicle on the side of the highway, that's why. Besides which, I'd rather change the tire with you out of the van. I want you both up there on that bank," he said firmly, pointing to the grassy hill outside the window. "Come on. Up. Get your coats."

"It's raining, Holt," Libby protested. "We'll get soaked."

"So will I," he reminded her with a snap in his voice. Evidently the patience he called up when dealing with his daughter didn't extend to her. He raked a hand through his hair and stood up abruptly. In a half crouch under the low roof, he made his way to them. "Scoot over," he ordered. They scooted. "I have a poncho back here somewhere," he said as he searched behind the seat and came up with a square of folded vinyl. "You can sit on one end and pull the other over your heads. You won't get too wet."

Libby suddenly remembered her small car. "Will you have to unhitch my car before you can change the tire?"

"No. Now come on, both of you, out."

The rain was light but cold. Libby pulled the child into the crook of her arm to warm her. Mercifully she was quiet as they huddled together under the poncho. What a miserable time and place to have a flat tire. They sat on the only patch of green in sight. The rest of the ground around them had been gouged to prepare for construction of additional lanes, the red clay beneath, slick and muddy, running like rivers of blood. Libby shivered and cuddled Jill closer.

Holt's hair was plastered to his head after only a few minutes, while his sheepskin jacket grew darker and heavier with the amount of water it absorbed. He unbuttoned it to give himself freedom to move more easily. The jack was new and stiff but sturdy, and in a short time he had the old tire off and the new one on. He tightened the lugs, replaced the hubcap and began to lower the van. All at once the jack slipped—the van bounced on its new tire. "Ouch! Dammit!" he yelped, slinging his hand down from his wrist. He yanked a handkerchief from his back pocket and wound it around his bloody thumb.

"What happened?"

"Did you hurt yourself, Daddy?"

He looked at the concern on the two faces as they scrambled down the bank toward him. Libby was dragging the poncho behind her. He forced himself to shrug off their sympathy, which took no little amount of effort. "I just pinched my thumb. It'll be okay."

"Don't be silly," said Libby, taking his forearm. "You're bleeding. Let me see." She unwound the white linen square.

He looked down at her bent head and smiled mockingly, though the thumb was throbbing like hell. "Why don't we get out of the rain and then you can look at it?" he said over the noise of the cars speeding by.

"That's a good idea." She dropped his hand to open the sliding door. "Hop in, Jill. You, too," she told Holt.

"I have to put away the tools and tire. You get in."

"Can't we just put them in the back for now? You really need that wound cleaned out. And it's raining. And you're soaked."

"I guess so." He heaved the tire in with his good hand, and Libby scooped up the tools. In seconds they were back inside. Holt had started the engine to get the heat going.

"Here's Daddy's first-aid kit, Libby. Daddy, did you cut your thumb *off*? Let me see."

Holt chuckled at Jill's ghoulishness. With his daughter's help Libby got the wound cleaned and antiseptic applied. Jill had the honor of putting on a bandage— to keep the germs out and the medicine in, she told him.

"Thanks, squirt. You'll make a great doctor or nurse someday."

"Why don't you let me drive for a while?" Libby asked.

"I'm fine," he scoffed. But driving wasn't as easy as he would have them believe. The wound extended to the small wing of flesh between thumb and forefinger, just where he gripped the steering wheel, so that every time he made an adjustment in direction it throbbed harder. He'd had broken bones that hurt less.

"Real men don't eat quiche," said Libby. She had returned to the swivel seat beside him. Jill was watching television.

"What?"

"Or admit to being in pain."

"I'm not in pain," he declared.

"Really?" she questioned mildly. "Then why is the muscle in your jaw jumping?"

"Well, it hurts a little," he admitted in a drawl.

She barked with laughter that wasn't laughter at all, making him grin at her.

"It beats me why some men can't admit to having feelings and vulnerabilities just like anyone else."

"Oh, I have feelings. Would you like to know what I was feeling just before the tire blew?" He lowered his voice suggestively.

She cocked her head, and her lips curved in the beginnings of a smile. "What?"

"I was feeling frustrated that we still had three hours to go to get to Macon, and then I had to feed Jill and bathe her and put her to bed before we could be alone. Before I could hold you and kiss you, caress your beautiful breasts and feel your naked body under mine."

"Holt!" The protest sounded breathless even to her ears.

"I figure that admission makes me pretty vulnerable."

"And prone to say things at the most inappropriate times," she informed him tersely.

"Yeah."

Fortunately Jill asked a question from the back seat, saving Libby from having to comment further. But even during spurts of conversation, Libby's thought returned to linger over the mental picture he painted, off and on until they reached the outskirts of Macon.

In contrast to Atlanta, the city was like a sleepy younger sister. When they exited from the highway to search for the hotel, it was after six o'clock and pitch-dark.

A tired, touchy Jill had begun to whine. "How much farther?" she demanded for the hundredth time. Libby had exhausted all her distracting ploys. It seemed the only thing that would satisfy the cranky child was dinner and bed.

Holt handed Libby the paper with the scrawled directions he'd been given over the telephone. "We'll be there in a few minutes, sweetheart."

"How long is a few?"

"Turn right at the next corner," instructed Libby.

"Daddy, I'm hungry."

"Are you sure?" he questioned Libby. "This looks more like a residential neighborhood."

"I think I'm sure. The sign back there said Maple Street." They drove another block. The street narrowed drastically.

"Are we lost, Daddy?" asked Jill in a fearful voice.

"No, squirt, we're not lost," Holt reassured her, but he was fast losing his composure.

"I thought you said we wouldn't get lost if Libby navigated."

"That's Maple *Drive*, not Maple Street," said Holt, indicating another green-lettered sign on the corner. "Now where the hell am I going to turn around?"

Evidently he meant the question to be rhetorical, because he slammed the van into reverse. The tires bumped against the curb, jolting them. Jill had been standing in the aisle between their chairs, and she sat down hard. She began to cry.

"Jill." Holt drew the word out forebodingly.

"Holt! Can't you hold on to your temper? Besides, you shouldn't be cursing in front of this child." Libby picked Jill up to cuddle her while trying again to decipher the riddle of the directions. "I can't read this word."

"We're lost!" wailed Jill.

"We're not lost, sweetheart."

"Holt, your handwriting is worse than a doctor's."

"I want my Nana!"

Holt slammed on the brakes. "Quiet!" he roared.

Jill swallowed her cries on a gulp. Libby looked at him, slack-jawed.

"That's better," he said in a thoroughly disgusted, rigidly controlled tone. "Now. I am going to get you to the hotel as soon as it is humanly possible to do so. Until then I would appreciate it if you would both shut up. Let me have the directions."

Silently Libby handed over the crumpled paper.

"Thank you." He turned on a small spotlight above his head and studied the hand-drawn map, the jerk of the muscle in his jaw belying his composure. "You're right, my handwriting is abominable," he finally admitted sheepishly. "I'm sorry I yelled."

"That's quite all right," Libby answered in a stiff tone.

Holt studied her unyielding profile for a minute. Without another word he folded the paper, tucked it into his breast pocket and put the van in gear.

Ten minutes later they were parked in the circular drive at the entrance to the hotel, bellmen unloading their luggage, a doorman assisting Jill and Libby from the front seat and a manager type escorting them through the swinging glass doors.

Ten minutes after that they were sitting down to order dinner, and an hour later a totally exhausted Jill fell asleep as soon as her head touched the pillow.

"Nashville seems a million miles away," murmured Libby on a yawn as she curled up on the bed in the next room. The voice of the television announcer was a mumble in the background.

She wore a peach-colored satin nightshirt that ended high on her thighs. It had inspired a long and satisfying, if scratchy, kiss, so that Holt was standing at the mirror in the bathroom shaving. His back was to her, but he met her eyes in the mirror and smiled. "It does, doesn't it? At times today, I wished we'd never left."

"I don't blame you. Your temper took a beating, didn't it?"

He had taken off his shirt, but still wore his jeans. Her eyes took pleasure from exploring his broad bare shoulders, his lean hips, the reflection of his masculine, hair-covered chest. She shivered, wishing he would hurry. She wanted his warmth. "How's your thumb?" she asked, and yawned again. Her eyelids were heavy. She'd just rest them a minute....

The next thing she knew Holt was standing over her, shaking her shoulder. Confused, she looked up at his somber expression. The lines in his face were pronounced, an indication that he was seriously worried. She sat up, alarmed. "What is it?"

"The weather, honey. I heard the report and then called home. There's a forecast of a freeze line south to Fort Lauderdale. We have to leave."

"Now? But, Holt, you're worn out."

Holt ran a hand around the back of his neck, massaging the tense muscles there. She was absolutely right. He was tired, but his crew had been cut to a bare skeleton during the holidays so that those of them who had families in other places could travel.

When he'd called home, his foreman had reported that some of the men had returned of their own volition when they heard the news of the weather—but not enough to handle both the cattle operation and the smudge pots that would have to be set out in hopes of saving the groves. Luckily his grove was situated on high ground and surrounded by lakes. The temperature and humidity from the water often kept his grove from freezing when all those around him did.

He tried to explain some of this to Libby as they packed. "But I've still got to get back. We don't know how low the temperature will drop."

"Then I insist you let me drive part of the way."

"Have you had any experience driving a van?" he asked guardedly. By now, he knew better then to allow his doubt to show.

"No, but my brother had a heavy-duty pickup truck when he was in college, and I drove that. I'm perfectly capable."

She was all business. "You won't be any good to your foreman if you're exhausted when you get there."

"You haven't had any more sleep than I have in the past two nights," he reminded her.

"But I napped in the van," she reminded him. "Please."

He finally gave in, but to Libby's mind it wasn't a gracious surrender.

Damn all macho men, she thought, but she didn't say anything as she hurried into the room where Jill was sleeping and began to gather up her clothes.

Holt went down to the desk to check them out; he returned with a sleepy bellman. The man carried the luggage and Holt carried Jill, still sleeping, to the van. Libby, dressed haphazardly but warmly in jeans and a yellow bulky sweater, hurried on ahead to open up the bed for the child.

Hopefully, Jill would sleep all the way. Holt was distracted. Coping with an irritable child wouldn't help.

She buckled herself into the driver's seat while Holt tipped the man and slammed his door. He tapped the dashboard sharply. "Okay, let's go," he said tersely.

She was a competent driver, though the pull of her car was a hindrance that took some getting used to. She had to concentrate. Gradually she began to relax and could feel Holt doing the same in the seat beside her. She tossed him a grin. "Didn't think I could do it, did you?" she teased.

"I never doubted you for a minute," he said innocently.

She hooted.

He chuckled, a deep, satisfied sound that sent chills of regret down her spine. If only they'd had time to make love once more. She didn't know what circumstances would be when they reached their destination, or how long it would be before they saw each other again. She was sure there were women in his life. A man like Holt probably had dozens.

LIBBY DROVE UNTIL TWO-THIRTY in the morning. She wasn't really that tired herself and didn't mind driving. In fact, it gave her a strange feeling of comfort to know she could do something for Holt. He had done so much for her—she would have been a human snowman somewhere on the highway north of Nashville if it hadn't been for him. Then he had stayed with her, sharing the holiday season in a hotel, when he could have left her alone. She wouldn't have thought any the worse of him.

Holt straightened in his seat and stretched his arms over his head in a parody of waking—when in truth, she knew he'd been half-awake all along.

"If you want to start looking for a gas station, we can fill up, then I'll drive for a while."

"Okay." She took her eyes off the road only long enough to smile at him. "Did the rest help?"

He grinned. "More than you know. I feel like a different person, but how about you? Are you sinking?"

"No, I'm fine."

The van topped a slight rise, rare in the flatlands of North Florida, and she saw an exit ahead. "I hope this station is open. Do you see any lights?"

"There's usually at least one open all night at each exit."

There were two, and Holt directed her toward the one that also housed a truck stop. "They always have the best coffee," he explained. "I could use a cup, couldn't you?"

"Is that why you stopped at a truck stop in Indianapolis?" she asked, thinking of the turn of fate that had brought them together. A chance meeting that had changed her life forever. No matter what happened between them from here on, she would never be the same.

His mind must have been running along the same path, because he answered in a reminiscent, tender tone. "I hate to give credit for such a momentous event to such a small item as a cup of coffee, but yes. Why did you happen to stop there?"

Libby shoved the gearshift into park and turned off the engine before facing him. She knew her eyes reflected the wonder she'd heard in his tone. "It was the only credit card I have," she said huskily.

Holt cupped the back of her neck in his big hand and pulled her toward him. Just before his mouth covered hers, he whispered, "Thank God."

The gentleness and reverence in the kiss brought the sting of tears to her eyes. His mouth was mobile over hers, tasting her carefully and thoroughly, but he didn't try to deepen the kiss. It was enough to be close, to share, for now.

Even through his weariness, his worry about his business, Holt's heart felt as though it would drown with love for this beautiful woman. He told himself to be cautious, on guard against frightening her away.

But, Lord, he *needed* her. Needed her warmth, her support, her love.

"How long do I have to wait, Libby?" he asked, hearing the hoarseness in his voice and hating the entreaty there.

He felt her immediate withdrawal.

"Don't, please," Libby choked, letting her eyes do the pleading for her. Try to understand, she begged silently. She couldn't, not until she was sure, sure that the feelings would last, that he wasn't going to do a turn around when he realized she wasn't cut out for the domestic role. "I don't want this! My job—"

"Yes, the job," he grated. "So what will we have?" he said, sadly bitter. "A night here and there and a rush home in the morning to get dressed before work? Maybe Jill could start calling you Aunt Libby; I know that her mother has brought a few 'uncles' home to spend a night or two." His bitterness erupted full force. He made an effort to tamp it down one more time. "I don't want you just in my bed, Libby. I want you in my life, as well. What can I do to prove that to you?"

"You can give me time," she said bluntly.

Holt heaved a sigh that seemed to come from the depths of his soul. "You ask a hell of a lot," he said heavily. "I love you. I need you now. Not sometime in the vague, unforeseeable future. Now!"

"I'm not ready, and I'm not convinced you are, either."

"What the hell do I have to do to convince you?"

She gripped the steering wheel and stared out through the windshield, seeing nothing, responding as though by rote. "Give me time."

"We know each other better than most couples. Look how much time we've spent together."

Her jaw became even firmer. "You're being unreasonable."

Holt recalled her remark about real men with a wry inward smile. Real men could be hurt. "Yeah, it's a failing of mine that you'd better be aware of. If I can't see the logic in an argument, I become very unreasonable. Do you love me?"

She nodded. "But it's not enough."

Holt jerked open the door of the van. Just before stepping to the ground he fixed her with his blue gaze, icy now and cold all the way to the soul of him. He didn't doubt her honesty. She loved him. But she didn't want the responsibility of a ready-made family. That had to be it. He sighed heavily. Could he really blame her for feeling that way? No, but he could regret her feelings, grieve over what they might have had together. "Maybe it never will be enough," he said tonelessly.

"Maybe not," she whispered.

11

AS THE COLD FRONT MOVED IN, in temperatures dropped slowly from the high thirties, but the thrust of the storm was still to arrive, at about four o'clock that afternoon. Then the thermometers would drop sharply to below freezing. Citrus growers all over the state were doing what they could to prepare, but many millions of dollars' worth of grapefruit and tangerines, oranges and tangelos, were expected to be lost.

"Are you sure you won't stay with us? There's plenty of room, and you'll be free to come and go as you wish." Holt's tone was controlled, cold and formal.

Libby met it with a voice that was equally calm, equally formal. "Thank you, Holt, but no. You'll be busy, and I need to start looking for a place of my own as soon as possible."

"Of course."

Libby had a thought. "Unless you need me—" She broke off when his eyes cut to her.

Her mind felt as if it had been put through the food processor. Lack of sleep must be the problem. "To—to stay with Jill," she added hurriedly.

"I don't need a baby-sitter. I've already arranged for someone to take care of Jill."

Libby turned from the irritation in his voice. He wasn't even trying to understand. Her eyes focused on the countryside flying past the window. Weak, early-morning sunlight made a valiant effort to warm the air outside, but she knew it was colder than it looked out there.

The radio had kept them informed about the progress of the cold front that was moving relentlessly toward south-central Florida, and for the past two hours they had been traveling through the area. They could see for themselves the measures that were being taken. Some growers were spraying water over the fruit trees in hopes of insulating them with a sheet of ice before the freeze came; others relied on the old faithful "smudge pots" that burned throughout the night in the groves, in hopes of keeping the trees alive.

When they left the interstate for the last time, Libby felt both relief and melancholy—relief that she no longer had to look at miles and miles of multilane traffic, yet depressed that her promising future had turned heels over applecart. She hadn't the least idea how to right it again without giving in. Was she making the biggest mistake of her life? She had suffered because of her stubborn nature before.

"This motel is new," Holt told her as he steered between two massive stuccoed pillars. "And convenient to where you'll be working. TOLTOT is straight down this road about a mile." His tone was clipped, impatient.

Libby knew he was anxious to be on his way and chastised herself for feeling hurt at his brusqueness.

What else did she expect? "I'm sure it will be fine," she answered quietly, looking around.

The entrance was Spanish in style, a red-tiled roof, arched openings along a shady walled passage. Plantings of palmetto, feather palms and cabbage ferns lined the walks; cypress and juniper trees threw shadows across the lawns. Even in the chill light of dawn it had an inviting air.

The moment Libby had been dreading was here. As soon as Holt stopped the van, Jill began to stir. Libby cringed from this goodbye as much as from any she had ever endured.

Jill had awakened only once during the long ride from Macon. Disoriented and confused, she had begun to cry softly. Libby had soothed her with the promise that they would soon be home, which had seemed to pacify her. Now she sat up among the tumbled covers and whimpered softly.

Libby glanced at Holt. "Shall I—"

"No," he interrupted. "I'll see to her. You go inside and make your arrangements. Then we'll unload."

And be on our way, Libby finished for him. Suddenly, under his waiting gaze, she felt clumsy and confused. She tried to hook the strap of her purse over her shoulder, but it kept falling down her arm. Finally, she gave up, fumbled with the door handle, opened it and jumped out of the van, glad to be away from that accusatory stare even briefly. Damn him, he had no right to make her feel guilty.

When she returned a few minutes later with a key in her hand, she had regained her composure. She climbed back inside the van and smiled with determination at the two of them. Jill was curled up securely in her father's lap, but her tear-stained cheeks attested to her unhappiness. He kept his arm around her as he started the engine and eased the van forward.

Her room was at the rear of the complex. Holt frowned as he followed her directions. "You shouldn't be stuck way back here. Who would hear you if you called for help?"

Libby forced a laugh to hide the dismay she was feeling on the same subject. It did look rather deserted. Only one other car was parked anywhere near. "I'll be fine. The clerk said these are the rooms they assign to rent by the week, rather than by the night. Besides, who knows, I may be lucky and find an apartment right away."

Bags unloaded, her car unhooked and parked in its designated spot...the moment Holt dreaded had arrived. He stood at the door of her room, holding his daughter securely in one arm, and looked around. Now that the time for parting had come, he was reluctant to leave. He had to go. His business waited, and every minute could mean the difference between the survival or death of a part of his livelihood.

Still, he had this horrible premonition that if he left, he might never see her again. His mind told him the thought was ridiculous, but his heart didn't listen. What would happen now, he wondered, schooling his expression not to reveal his feelings.

Libby was a beautiful woman, and beautiful women were never alone for long. She would find someone else, someone who didn't have the responsibilities he had. Had he wanted to, there was no way he could compete with freedom. She had made it clear she wanted to be left alone, so that was exactly what he would do.

He opened his mouth to speak, but she plunged in first. "Holt, I want to thank you for everything." She gave a little laugh and looked away. "Thanks is such an ineffectual word."

"No thanks are necessary, Libby. Not between us." He held out one hand, palm up, and she placed hers in it. He bent to touch her lips lightly, but they acted as a magnet, drawing him into a kiss deeper than he had intended. Desire rose in him like a tide. The child in his arms made a small sound. With a wrench he pulled his mouth away. "Goodbye, Libby," he said hoarsely.

His daughter's small body stiffened. "No!" Jill cried on a harsh sob. "No, don't say that! I hate that word!" She burst into tears. "I hate goodbye!" She buried her face in his neck.

Libby blinked at the tears in her own eyes. Poor baby. There had been enough goodbyes in her young life. Her mother, her Nana—how could she be expected to understand? "Jill, sweetheart, this is not really goodbye. We'll see each other." Helplessly she soothed the small back with her hand.

Jill withdrew sharply from her touch. "Don't. I don't think I'm going to love you anymore, so don't touch me."

Libby jerked back her hand as though she'd been burned. "I hope you don't mean that, Jill," she said quietly. "It would make me very sad if you didn't love me."

"Well, I won't," the child said stubbornly.

Libby knew the girl was tired and very upset, but her words cut to the soul. She met Holt's gaze with eyes that now spilled their own tears of exhaustion. "Oh, Holt..." she whispered. "I wouldn't hurt her for anything."

He squeezed her shoulder reassuringly, but his eyes had a powerless look. "She knows that, Libby. Please don't cry. Libby, *please!*"

The poor man looked as torn as Libby felt, and no wonder—two hysterical people on his hands. She forced a smile to her lips, even managed a laugh—of sorts. "Go on, take her home. I'll be fine." The words came out more roughly than she had intended.

"I'll call you," he grated, and spun on his heel to stride toward the van.

When? thought Libby, but she didn't say it.

WHEN, SHE WAS STILL WONDERING three days later. She wouldn't have believed she could miss anyone as she missed Holt and Jill. In a short time they had both become so important to her that even the bright warm sunshine of her new home state couldn't melt the icy premonition around her heart; she had made a gigantic mistake.

The storm had raged for a violent twenty-four hours, sweeping away two lives and millions of dollars' worth of property. She had watched its progress on the small television in her room. But two more days had passed since the end of the storm, and she still hadn't heard from Holt.

It was New Year's Eve day. Libby had made arrangements to meet with the real-estate agent, Rose Landin, at ten o'clock. They had spent seven hours together yesterday, discussing Libby's needs and viewing property. So far, the woman had come up with nothing that Libby liked, but a quick friendship had developed between them. Rose had insisted that she didn't mind working on what would have been a holiday for her and had agreed to show Libby two more condominiums on her list.

Libby dressed in a lightweight khaki poplin suit with a coral cotton blouse, once more marveling that less than a week ago she had been caught in a snowstorm. She wound her hair into a loose topknot, darkened her lashes with a dab of mascara and touched her lips with a coral gloss. Her skin was so pale in comparison to the Floridians she had met that she used a heavy hand with the blusher.

When she had finished she examined herself critically in the mirror. Something was definitely amiss. She bent forward from the waist for a closer look. There it was—a sadness around the eyes, a droop to the mouth. *And what do you have to feel sad and droopy about?* she asked herself sternly. *You have a wonderful new job in a beautiful city; you're on your own, freer than you've ever been, and isn't that what you wanted?*

A knock at her door startled her out of her reverie. "Coming!" she called. She turned off the lamp on the dresser and picked up her purse from the bed. "Hi, Rose."

"Good morning, Libby." The older woman smiled. "Ready to hit the streets?"

"Ready." Libby checked in her purse to make sure she had her key and closed the door. Just then the telephone rang.

Holt! Libby was electrified into action, not stopping to ask herself how she knew. Where was the blasted key? She'd just had her hand on—ah, here. She fumbled, trying to insert it upside down, but finally got the door open on the fourth ring. The phone was on the table between the two beds. As she raced for it she banged her shin on the corner of one. "Damn! Ouch! Hello!" The last word was uttered in the softest, most appealing of tones.

"I was about to decide you were out," Holt said evenly.

"Five seconds more and I would have been. The real-estate agent is taking me to look at condos this morning." She kept her voice at a casual level.

"I won't keep you but a minute."

"That's all right, Holt. I—I'm glad to hear from you." Glad? She was ecstatic. She couldn't keep the crazy grin off her face.

Rose turned away politely, but the set of her shoulders indicated she was listening to every word. Libby didn't care.

"How are you, Libby?"

Though he spoke noncommittally, though he was reserved, he sounded so *good*. She closed her eyes briefly. "I'm fine. How are you?" Commonplace platitudes, but knowing he was there on the other end of the line lifted her spirits drastically. She wondered if they were going to pussyfoot around each other during the whole conversation.

"Okay." He chuckled tiredly. "Now that the sun is shining again. Would you believe I just realized this is New Year's Eve?"

"How is everything? Did you suffer much damage from the storm? And how is Jill?" The questions tumbled out over each other.

This time his laughter seemed easier, more natural. "I'll answer all your questions tonight, if you'll see in the new year with me. I know it's late notice, but I hope you haven't made other plans."

She hesitated, not wanting Holt to feel responsible for her just because she was a newcomer to the area.

"I don't have any plans, but please don't think you have to entertain me."

"Dammit, Libby," he snapped. "You know better than that. Do you want to go out or not?"

"Yes."

He sighed audibly. "Good. The country club is having a dinner dance. Black tie. I'll pick you up at eight."

"I'll be ready."

She was about to replace the receiver when his voice stopped her. "Hey!"

"Yes, Holt?"

"Don't wear that dress," he said gruffly.

Libby didn't have to ask what dress he meant. "Okay." She hung up the telephone and stood looking down at it for a full minute, lost in her thoughts. She was recalled to the present by Rose, clearing her throat.

"I couldn't help overhearing, Libby. Was that Holt Whitney?"

"Yes. Do you know him?"

"This is a small town. Everyone knows everyone else. But, yes. Holt and my husband and I all grew up together."

"He invited me out for New Year's Eve."

"I didn't realize you knew him."

"We met..." Her voice trailed off. How on earth did you explain that you'd met someone in a truck stop on the interstate? Finally she shrugged. "It's a long story."

Rose seemed to settle for that, but Libby could see that her curiosity was piqued.

"It really is a long story," she said with a smile of apology.

"But you know each other well?"

This time Libby's smile was private. "You could say that, yes."

"I'd like to hear the story someday when we have plenty of time. Holt is a very lonely man."

"Lonely? I didn't get that impression."

"Oh, he's been breaking hearts around here for as long as I can remember, but deep down he was left quite embittered by his marriage. He doesn't really trust women all that much. I hope that having his daughter with him will help. Have you met Jill, too?"

Libby was surprised. She speculated on Rose's revelations and decided she was glad she'd never seen the embittered side of Holt. "Yes, I know her," she said quietly.

Rose finally seemed to get the message that her client didn't want to discuss Holt Whitney or his daughter. "Are you all going to the New Year Eve's party at the country club by any chance?"

"Yes." Libby was relieved to talk about something else. Her feelings for Holt and Jill were too raw to discuss and the promise of seeing him again, too personal. "Will you be there, too?"

Rose nodded. "Maybe we can have a drink together. You can meet my husband."

"I'd like to meet Lex."

"Fine. Now let's go. I think you are really going to love this first place I have to show you. It seems to have everything you're looking for, and it's close to TOLTOT."

The condominium wasn't quite right. Libby couldn't put her finger on just exactly what she didn't like about it. The next one Rose showed her didn't even come close. She was grateful for Rose's patience. She sighed. "Rose, I apologize for getting you out on a holiday. I don't seem to be able to make up my mind about anything."

"Don't worry," said the older woman kindly. "We've only been looking for two days. Sometimes it takes weeks to find a suitable place." But Libby didn't miss Rose's quizzical look.

She could hardly expect Rose to understand her hesitation when she didn't understand it herself. She normally wasn't hard to please. The condominiums were lovely; actually, the first one they'd seen had all the particular features she had insisted she wanted. Freshly painted, it was ready for occupancy. The price was right. She could have moved in immediately. So why was it so difficult to make a decision?

Because her mind wasn't on condos. Her mind was on Holt Whitney and the evening to come. "We'll try again in a few days," she said finally. "Right now I need another kind of advice."

"What is it?"

"Where can I buy a knockout dress to wear to-night?"

Rose grinned, her brown eyes sparkling with delight. "I know just the place. Come on."

LIBBY PAUSED at the top of the stairs and looked down over the throng of well-dressed people in the dining room below. One end of the room had been left clear for dancing, but as yet the bandstand was empty.

As she glanced around at women in elegant gowns of every color and style, Libby was especially glad she'd gone shopping. The long, slim ivory skirt was split up the side to her knee, and the separate sleeveless top was lightly beaded in the same color. Fashioned of soft crepe, the gown was almost weightless. She had scooped her hair to one side and anchored the fall with an ivory comb.

Holt looked magnificent in evening clothes, she thought again as she turned to look up at him. But his face still showed the ravages of the exhaustive few days he'd had. She hoped fatigue also accounted for the strange formality with which he'd greeted her.

He hadn't been to bed until yesterday, apparently, at which point he'd slept the clock around. He also assured her after only a heartbeat's hesitation that Jill was fine. The woman he had hired was working out very well.

"The club is lovely," she said. "Thank you for bringing me."

"I'm glad you could come," he answered with perfect politeness that was like a blade piercing Libby's heart. "Shall we look for Lex and Rose?" He indicated that she should precede him down the few steps to the dining-room level.

Holt hadn't even tried to hide his relief when she had mentioned that her real-estate agent was a friend of his. That was the first hint of warmth she'd seen in his eyes, though she couldn't fault his manners. "Maybe we can find a table together."

Agreeing readily, she hid her disappointment that he didn't seem to want to be alone with her.

"Fine."

Rose was standing at the entrance to the lounge, a rangy blond man beside her. When she spied Holt and Libby, she waved.

Libby led the way through the tables toward them. They were stopped twice by friends of Holt's. He performed the introductions with conventional decorum, but she caught some of the people they passed eyeing her speculatively.

"Libby, I want you to meet my husband, Lex," said Rose as they approached. "Darling, this is Libby Hamilton."

Holding out her hand, Libby responded warmly to the tall man's smile, until she realized it didn't quite reach his eyes. Amid the rush of greetings, she managed to conceal her dismay at the hostility she saw there. Rose was so warm, so friendly; what reason could Rose's husband have for being antagonistic? Lex shook hands with Holt; Holt kissed Rose's cheek. By that time Libby once again had control of herself.

"How about sharing a table for dinner?" Holt asked. "Or are you meeting someone?"

"No, we weren't sure until today whether we could make it or not," said Lex without further explanation.

Libby was grateful for Rose's presence during dinner. She hadn't realized that Holt was the president of the county growers' association until the older woman told her. Luckily this area hadn't been hit as hard as the counties fifty miles north, but there had been damage. The main topic of discussion was the storm and its aftereffects, the conversation interrupted frequently by other growers who stopped by their table to say hello to Holt or ask advice.

He made sure Libby had everything she needed, he was a perfect escort, but the evening was turning into a rather prosaic date.

"More coffee?—No, thank you," was just about the extent of their dialogue during the meal.

The puzzle of Lex's hostility was solved when Libby and Rose made a trip to the ladies' room. "I'm sorry Lex is being such an ass, Libby," Rose apologized. "I happened to mention that you were excited about your new job, and he decided you shouldn't be dating Holt."

Libby almost choked.

"You see, Holt's first wife was a woman who was strongly career minded...."

At that point Libby tuned her new friend out, but nodded at intervals while Rose chattered on. She could just imagine the conversation that had taken place. Holt certainly had loyal friends...and snoopy, meddling ones.

When the band took their places after dinner, Holt turned to her. "Would you like to dance?"

"Yes, I certainly would," she said resolutely. She was beginning to wonder why he had asked her here in the first place. She intended to find out.

But when he took her in his arms, he also took the wind out of her sails. "I'm sorry for all the interruptions."

Her gaze met his, and fell. "That's all right," she said weakly. The warmth of his arm across her back, his fingers intertwined with hers, the familiar tangy scent of his after-shave—all were having their effect on her senses, bringing back the memory of the night they had danced in the living room of the farmhouse outside Nashville. But this wasn't the same at all. Then he had held her like a lover, now he held her like a friend. Nashville might have been another world.

Holt looked down at Libby's lashes curled softly against her cheek. She smelled like summer daisies, and when her breasts brushed his chest, his fingers involuntarily tightened around her slender hand. He had to fight a battle within himself to keep from throwing her over his shoulder and disappearing into the night with her. He retreated slightly.

This hadn't been the best idea, bringing her here. He had thought that surrounded by people he would be able to keep his desires under control. It hadn't worked out that way. He was so aware of her every move, her every expression, that he'd barely been able to give coherent answers to the questions he'd been asked by his friends and fellow growers. As a result he had become more and more short-tempered.

Libby felt his physical withdrawal and finally decided she couldn't take this any longer. "Holt?" she began quietly.

He drew back slightly. "Libby?"

Her smile was an effort, when what she wanted to do was shake him. "Would you mind taking me home?"

A blue-white flame was lit in his eyes. "Home?" he asked, holding his breath.

"I mean back to the motel."

He let the air out of his lungs slowly. "Certainly," he said. "Would you mind telling me why?"

Because this is a mistake, because you're not the same man I thought I knew. You're a stranger. "Because I obviously cramp your style," she told him.

Holt dropped his arms in surprise, and she took advantage to move away from him. A glimmer of amusement lit in his eyes. A ray of hope poked through his dark mood as he watched her proud straight back.

The table was empty. Holt joined her, looking around. "Rose and Lex are dancing. Do you want to wait to say good-night?" he asked her.

"If you don't mind."

"Not at all," he said, seating her, then himself. He reached for his drink. "I'm really sorry I haven't been very attentive to you."

Her hair swung forward to fall over her breast as her head whipped around to face him. "Is that why you think I want to leave? Because I feel neglected?"

He didn't answer, but his expression said enough.

Her anger grew to meet his indifference. "Holt, do you realize you haven't smiled—not once—this whole evening?"

He looked blank. "Smiled?"

"Not once," she repeated irritably.

Holt studied her in silence for a long minute. "Look, Libby—"

"Whew," said Rose as she plopped into her seat. "It's so crowded out there that togetherness is a foregone conclusion. I see you two gave up. I don't blame you."

Libby picked up her purse and stood. "Holt is going to take me home, but I wanted to say good-night. It's been a pleasure meeting you, Lex." She could hardly keep the sarcasm out of her voice, and the man had the grace to look embarrassed. "Rose, I'll see you in a couple of days."

Rose put a hand on Holt's sleeve to check him as he started to rise. "Is it Jill? Is she worse, Holt?"

"Worse?" said Libby, suddenly alarmed. "Worse than what? Has she been sick?"

Holt patted Rose's hand and disentangled himself. "She's fine now." He turned to Libby. "Jill had a cold— but she's over it," he explained.

"Why. . .?" *Why didn't you call me?* she had started to say, her indignation rising. Then she realized she had no right to demand an answer. No right at all. Jill wasn't hers. "Are you sure she's all right?" she murmured. *Did she ask for me?* she wanted to add.

She waited until they were in the car before questioning him further. "Did you take her to the doctor?"

"Of course I did," Holt said tersely. He added with awful finality. "The cold developed into bronchitis. But she is completely well now."

"Why didn't you call me?" Libby was horrified that the child she loved could be that sick without her knowledge. Her throat closed around the words, but he heard.

"Jill is no worry of yours, Libby. You wanted it that way, and that's the way it is. Besides, I had my hands full; I didn't have time to call anyone except the doctor."

The accusation in his voice put a period to any further conversation. But the dialogue continued inside her head. *You needed me. That's what you said. And I didn't listen. I should have, but I was too damned stubborn, too afraid of being tied down to understand. You and Jill needed me, and I wasn't there because my timetable didn't coincide with yours. Will you ever forgive me, Holt?*

The light above the door to her room cast a yellow pall over his features as Holt took her key from her and inserted it in the lock. He pushed the door open a crack and gave her back the key. "The evening wasn't such a great success, was it?" he asked quietly.

Libby swallowed the lump that burned in her throat, then shook her head. "I'm sorry," she said softly. *Sorry for spoiling your evening, sorry for not being there.* So this is the way it ends, she thought miserably, with a whimper, not a bang. She started to turn away.

Holt surprised her by taking her face in his hands. He searched her expression. One of his thumbs scraped lightly across her lips, numbing them. She thought his hands were trembling but couldn't be sure.

"Happy New Year, my love," he said softly, lowering his head.

At first he barely brushed her lips. She felt the shock all the way to her toes. Unbidden, her arms crept up to wind around his neck, and suddenly she was crushed against his hard length. His arms circled her back, threatening to cut off her air supply. His mouth opened hungrily over hers, devouring her taste as though it was the last he would ever have, and he wanted enough to last forever.

With a groan of anguish, he thrust her away from him and swung away. "Good night," he choked as he strode to the car. He didn't look at her again.

12

LIBBY CHANGED into a pair of jeans and a white tailored shirt, flipped on the television and toasted in the New Year with a can of cola from the dispensing machine down the hall.

The great lighted ball fell in Times Square, and the crowds cheered as optimistically as they did each year. A new chance, a new beginning, was heralded by tradition and celebration. Put the old worries behind you. A new day, a new start…. Libby jumped up from where she rested against the pillows and switched off the television. She began to pace.

"I hate goodbyes." Jill's words rang in Libby's ears, splitting the wall she had surrounded herself with. The wall was a defense against the demands of a suffocating family, but Holt wasn't like her family. The only thing he asked of her was that she be there when he needed her. He'd never demanded that she give up her job, though ambition had destroyed his first marriage. He hadn't asked her to give up anything, only to share her life with him and his daughter.

How could she have compared this relationship to the one she had with her family? They had never needed her. Holt did. They suffocated her by giving. Holt was willing to give—and take.

Jill. Libby's eyes flooded with tears as she thought of the child she loved, ill in a strange house, probably crying.... Both of them had needed her, and she hadn't been there. She could have smoothed the transition for Jill, nursed the child, held her when she cried, played with her when she grew restless. No wonder Holt had been restrained at the party. No wonder he hadn't argued when she wanted to go home.

That brief flare in his eyes when she had said the word, "home"—had he hoped she meant his home? She paused at the mirror, her hands jammed in the back pockets of her jeans, and stared at herself. What she wanted, more than anything in the world at this moment, was another chance. She couldn't turn the clock back, couldn't use her hindsight to undo the damage, but she could ask the man she loved for another chance.

She did love him. She had admitted that to herself long ago. On a conscious level, however, she had let her relationship with her family distort her view of marriage and family life.

All at once, she had to know if she'd killed it all, if he'd changed his mind. There was no more time to be wasted. She grabbed her purse and the car keys and left the lonely room, slamming the door decisively behind her.

At one-thirty Libby was driving the back roads outside town. Rose had indicated the general direction of Holt's house when they were out yesterday. Libby had been confident she could find it, but now she wasn't even confident she could find the main road again.

The night was moonless, black as tar, not a light from anywhere except her headlights. The potholes caught her small vehicle unawares and, in her haste, Libby bumped her head on the roof. "Ouch!" She slowed deliberately; all she needed now was a flat tire.

The glow of her headlights illuminated the ominous shadow of a huge building of some sort, off the road to her left. And a sight she would be forever grateful to see: a telephone cubicle.

But no telephone directory.

Libby bit back a word that would have shocked her mother and rooted through her purse for a quarter. She prayed the information operator wasn't out celebrating.

She waited for what seemed forever, until someone finally came on the line with her answer. "The number is five-five-five-oh-nine-five-one," said the recording.

"Wait! I don't have anything to write with!" Libby shouted into the receiver.

"Five-five-five-oh-nine-five-one," repeated the recording.

"Thanks," said Libby wryly. "Five-five-five-oh-nine-five-one." She recited it again so that she wouldn't forget as she punched in the numbers. "Oh-nine-five-one..."

"What...?" said a puzzled voice on the other end.

"Holt?"

"Libby?" Holt wondered if he was hearing things. He stared at the decorative mirror on the opposite wall of his study. It reflected a disheveled, distorted figure slumped in a chair, the wrinkled dress shirt open almost to the waist, the dangling ends of a black bow tie, the tousled hair, the eyes exaggeratedly wide. "Libby?"

he repeated softly, slowly straightening, setting down the brandy glass with a hand that shook violently.

"Yes, it's me." *Might as well plunge right in*, Libby told herself. "I, uh, I was wondering if you could forgive me."

"At two o'clock in the morning?" he said dryly.

"Oh, dear. Were you asleep? I'm sorry if I woke you up. But I didn't want to wait until tomorrow. I had to tell you right now. I love you, Holt, and I know you better than anyone, even if we only met two weeks ago." Her voice cracked; she had to take a breath before she could finish. "I was wrong to waste even a day of our time together, and if you can forgive me I'd like to come home to you and Jill."

"Two weeks and a day."

"What?"

"Nothing!" he exclaimed. "It isn't important, darling. Oh, Libby, of course I want you—we want you. Anytime. I love you. Do you hear me? I love you."

Nodding, she could hear the joy building in his voice. He sounded as crazy as she did, she thought lovingly as she brushed at the tears of happiness that wet her cheeks.

Holt's mind was already clicking with the practical, the mundane. Should he wake Jill's nurse? Or just leave? He could probably be back before anyone was aware he was gone. "Libby, stay there. I'll pick you up in ten minutes."

"Don't hang up!" she screamed into the phone. "Holt, are you there? I'm not at the motel."

"Calm down, honey. I'm here."

She tried to keep the frustrated hysteria out of her voice, but failed miserably. "I wanted to find you, come home, but unfortunately I can't find where home is."

"Where the hell *are* you?"

"I don't know. On a dirt road somewhere." She looked out helplessly at the darkness. "It's dark, and there's a big building."

Holt, on his feet now, raked a hand through his hair. He directed his brandy-fuzzed brain to function. Dammit! She could be anywhere! "A big building? Probably a citrus warehouse. Can you see a sign anywhere? Look on the front of the building."

Libby leaned out of the cubicle as far as the cord would allow. Her eyes had adjusted to the dark now, and she could see some letters. "W-H-I...Whitney's," she breathed.

She heard the phone clatter on the other end, even as her gaze traveled beyond the huge dark shape of the warehouse to the top of a hill behind it and centered on a large colonial house.

Almost before the echo of her whisper died, the front door of the house was flung open, spilling light out and silhouetting the large figure of a man.

He ran swiftly down the hill. Libby dropped the phone and ran, too, up the hill, along a corridor of trees, through the sweet-smelling orange trees, toward him, toward home.

Holt met her more than halfway down. He opened his arms and caught her close, swinging her around once before burying his face in the glorious cloud of her hair. "Libby, Libby, oh, my darling." His arms contracted, lifting her until their faces were level.

She met his smile with a grin and covered his face with kisses. "Can you. . .believe I found you without...knowing where I was? I feel like a homing pigeon."

He laughed and pulled her under his arm, heading back down the hill toward her car. "Did you pack, love? Did you check out of the motel?"

The sight of him took her breath away. He still wore his tuxedo pants and pleated shirt, but he had loosened the tie and the shirt was unbuttoned almost to his waist. He was the sexiest man she'd ever seen. "No. I didn't know whether you'd let me stay," she said when she could breathe again.

"Let you. . .?" he sputtered. "I'll get you for that." He lifted her off her feet for a quick kiss. "Never mind. I'll take care of it tomorrow. Tonight, or what's left of it, I have plans for you."

"Is that a promise?" she asked happily as they reached the car.

Holt slid in behind the wheel without asking, but Libby decided to ignore his presumption for now. She got in on the passenger side.

"That's a guarantee." And he started the engine.

The house was much larger up close than it had appeared from a distance. "Holt, it's beautiful," she murmured when he stopped the car at the foot of the steps.

He switched off the motor and turned to her. "I'm glad you like it." His finger curled tightly around her hand. "Don't worry that you'll have to keep it clean and work, too. I have a housekeeper who comes every day. She'll pick Jill up from nursery school and stay with her in the afternoons."

"Thank you," said Libby very softly, smiling at his thoughtfulness. He was reassuring her immediately that he didn't expect her to give up her career. They sat looking at each other, unwilling to break the eye contact for a quiet minute. "I love you so very much," Libby finally whispered.

"And I love you, more than anything in the world."

"Are you going to show me the house?"

He grinned. "Part of it."

"Let me guess." She laughed. "Your bedroom, right?"

"I knew you were a smart lady." He opened the door and came around to help her out. "Welcome home, my love." He scooped her up and carried her inside, giving the door a kick to shut it behind them. He didn't miss a step in his stride as he started up a wide winding staircase.

Her arms circled his neck. She tucked her face into his neck and nuzzled his chin. "Hey, you're getting ahead of yourself. You're not supposed to carry me over the threshold until after we're married."

When he reached the top of the stairs, he turned right and entered a large, beautifully proportioned bedroom. He set her on her feet beside a king-size bed. Sitting on the edge of the mattress, he pulled her between his legs. "I've felt married to you since the first time we made love, in Nashville," he said solemnly. "The ceremony will only be a formality as far as I'm concerned, my darling." He pressed his cheek to her stomach and held her, just held her.

Libby threaded her fingers through the hair at his nape, laid her cheek on top of his head. "I think I felt the same way, Holt, I just wouldn't admit it to myself.

You're so strong that you made me afraid I would lose myself in you."

"Darling, I don't want that. I fell in love with a beautiful, intelligent woman. And you're not another Linda."

"No, I'm not. I've never been obsessed with ambition, but I do enjoy my work."

"And you shall continue to work for as long as you like. Under one condition."

She drew back to look at him suspiciously, but he winked. "What's the condition?" she asked.

"You have to teach me how to work a computer. Jill thinks I'm a real dumbo, because I can't answer her questions."

Libby laughed in disbelief. "Do you mean your businesses aren't set up on computer?" she asked, unable to believe such a successful man was so behind the times.

"Nope. We do everything the old-fashioned way."

"Good heavens, Holt. You're operating in the dark ages. I can see I'll have to take you in hand."

"You can start tomorrow. I have other plans for tonight...." His hands at her back had begun a smoothing caress from her hands up her arms to her shoulders, then forward to cup her breasts. She inhaled as he squeezed gently. "Oh, my darling, I've missed you...and this," he groaned huskily, leaning forward to kiss the peaks through the fabric of her blouse. His hands shook slightly as he started to work on her buttons.

Libby's knees refused to support her any longer. She sat on his thigh and slipped her hand into his open shirt. His heart gave a leap under her fingers. His skin was warm, the hair there springy under her hand. "You feel good," she whispered, her lips playing across his ear. Deliberately she let her tongue follow.

The action had the effect of an explosion on him. The rest of her buttons flew right and left as he stripped the blouse off her shoulders and fumbled with the fastening of her jeans. In seconds he had her clothes off.

Libby laughed, a husky, seductive sound.

"You witch!" Holt groaned. "You know exactly how to get to me, don't you?" He wrapped his arms around her waist and twisted, landing her on the bed crosswise, kissing her long and deeply. Then he stood and stripped.

Libby watched through the screen of her lashes. At the sight of his aroused masculinity her body turned to liquid. The love that shone from the electric blue eyes reached out to her, demanding that she lower the final barrier, that she belong to him as completely as he belonged to her. She moaned softly and rolled away from the sight, her body trembling.

Too much, her mind cried. He affected her too much. The wave of love and desire that coursed through her took with it her breath, her senses, even the very heartbeat that kept her alive.

She became aware of his gentle touch, his palm lying warm on her spine. "Libby...darling...never too much."

She hadn't realized she'd spoken the words, and lifted her head. She didn't want him to misunderstand, to take her words as another denial. Through the curtain of her hair, she searched his face. "I know, my love. I didn't mean..."

He joined her on the bed, pulling her into his hard, warm embrace. "I know, too, my darling. The love, the emotions I feel for you are so powerful that I think I'm drowning."

"Yes," she whispered against his chest.

The big hands dove into her hair, lifting her face. He grinned in an attempt to slow the mood to a manageable pace; but his fingers shook; his breath was an uneven rasp. He closed his eyes briefly. "But what a way to go," he said in a hoarse, velvety voice.

Libby stretched up to cover his lips with hers. Then she was drowning, floating somewhere beneath the floodtide of passion and desire, drifting under the spell of his hands, the heated moistness of his mouth, everywhere on her. No one spot—not her swollen breasts, not the throbbing between her thighs, not the dark sweet cavern of her mouth—became the focus of sensation. Instead her entire being was one sweet, aching torment, begging to be filled.

Holt moved above her, burying his face in the scented cloud of her hair. She met his thrust with a welcoming shift of her hips. And then all sensation was concentrated on the force that drew them, together, across time and space to another dimension. Clinging frantically, bonded, they climbed to the infinite regions of experience...and drifted slowly, softly, as though borne on a feather, back into a world that was new and bright and filled with tomorrows.

Holt lifted his head to smile down at her, all the wonder in his eyes. "That was incredible," he whispered. "You're incredible."

"No more goodbyes, ever." Her eyes swam with tears. "I almost lost you...this."

"My darling, you never even came close."

"I didn't?"

He combed her golden hair with his fingers. "After we got here, the first night I mean, the world fell in on me. We hadn't parted on the best of terms—" he sighed "—and I was feeling down, anyway. Then the weather...the groves...Jill was miserable and sick. If I'd had the time to call, I doubt that I would have been pleasant or even coherent. You were right, my darling, when you called me unreasonable and demanding."

She put her fingers over his mouth. "No."

He turned her hand to leave a kiss in the palm and rolled to his side, keeping her close. His head fell back on the pillow. "But underneath it all, I was missing you like hell. I know tonight at the club was a disaster, but I was trying to give you the room I knew you needed."

"And I had discovered that I didn't need the room or time anymore. All I needed was you and Jill."

He tucked his chin into his chest to look down at her. "Are you sure?" he asked quietly.

She smiled, letting all the love she felt shine from her eyes. "I'm positive, and you know how stubborn I can be when I make up my mind."

THE HOUSE WAS DARK and Holt was sleeping deeply when Libby made her way into the hall. She tried three doors before she found the right one. A finger of moonlight touched the small figure in the center of the white canopied bed.

Libby smoothed the hair away from Jill's cool forehead and leaned over to kiss her cheek. The child stirred but didn't waken. *I'll be here for you*, she vowed silently. *From now on I'll be here.*

WONDERFUL SENSATIONS ENTICED LIBBY out of a dream. She opened her eyes to a room filtered with sunlight. A heavy arm over her waist tightened to bring her closer against a strong masculine chest. "Wake up," said Holt in a sleep-husky voice. His hand began a tender assault on her breasts.

"I'm awake," she murmured, turning to face him. "Happy New Year."

"Happy New Year, my love." He covered her lips with the gentlest of kisses. "Where do you want to go for a honeymoon?" There was a teasing light in his sharp blue eyes. "I have a place down on Key Largo. It's interstate all the way."

Libby groaned and started to laugh. "Absolutely not! I don't want to see another interstate for a long, long time." She put a forefinger in the center of his chest. "You listen to me, Holt Whitney. We're not going anywhere. We're staying right here, at home."

Holt rolled to his back, hauling her over his chest. His hand went to her nape to force her head down for a lingering kiss.

"Are you kissing *again*?" came the voice from the doorway.

They both turned their heads to look at the child who watched them soberly. In her long granny gown, her hair a mass of tangles, Jill nevertheless had a very serious, very guarded look on her face.

Holt tucked the covers around them more securely. He cleared his throat. "Libby and I will probably do a lot of kissing, sweetheart, when she marries me and comes to live with us. I hope it doesn't bother you."

Jill shrugged as though to say it didn't really matter to her, but her eyes were very bright.

Please don't cry, little love, thought Libby. An idea occurred to her then. "Of course, we'll need you to kiss us, too."

"Me?"

Libby nodded. "And you'll get tired of us kissing you."

Jill thought about that. "If I do, I'll just tell you to stop."

Holt swallowed a laugh. "Okay," he agreed.

Their minds working in unison, the two adults in the bed each held out an arm. Jill took a hesitant step, then another. All at once a wide smile dawned on her face. She reached them in one bound and was swept, giggling, into a tight embrace. "I've missed you, Libby. I'm so glad you're back. I didn't mean it when I said I didn't want to love you anymore."

"I was hoping you didn't." Libby smiled tenderly and hugged the child she couldn't love more if she had been born of her own body. "I was hoping you needed me enough to let me come back."

Jill looked at Libby, her brow furrowed, and Libby held her breath. Finally Jill smiled, her eyes wide and round. She didn't have to say anything.

Deeply moved, Holt closed his eyes and brought both of them into a hard embrace. He had his world right here in his arms.

THE AUTHOR

Georgia writer Marion Smith Collins has done everything from operating a gourmet tearoom to interior designing. But writing fiction is her greatest love, the one thing she wants to do every day for the rest of her life.

For recreation she and her husband enjoy water sports—"walking on the beach, floating on a rubber raft and sunbathing," says Marion. Her gentle humor is part of what makes her Temptations so appealing. Look for more from this popular author.

Harlequin Temptation

COMING NEXT MONTH

#89 THE WINGS OF MORNING
Jackie Weger

There was something about cocksure
Garrett Stark that really got under
Rachel Cameron's skin. And the feeling was
mutual. As County Sheriff, Garrett was tempted
to arrest her for disturbing his peace...

#90 LISTEN WITH YOUR HEART
Jane Edwards

Though Nicholas blamed himself for Casi's
blindness, Casi knew it had been an accident. His
stimulation of her other senses, however, was
definitely deliberate.

#91 TRUE COLORS Jayne Ann Krentz

Seeking out the man who'd once loved you, then
betrayed you, was no easy task. But Jamie
needed answers to the question burning in
her heart.

#92 AN IMPRACTICAL PASSION
Vicki Lewis Thompson

Mother Nature was hitting Sydney hard—how
could she contend with both a hurricane *and*
wild and sexy Colin Lassiter? Yet the last thing
she wanted to do was run for cover....

WORLDWIDE LIBRARY IS YOUR TICKET TO ROMANCE, ADVENTURE AND EXCITEMENT

Experience it all in these big, bold Bestsellers— Yours exclusively from WORLDWIDE LIBRARY WHILE QUANTITIES LAST

To receive these Bestsellers, complete the order form, detach and send together with your check or money order (include 75¢ postage and handling), payable to WORLDWIDE LIBRARY, to:

In the U.S.
WORLDWIDE LIBRARY
P.O. Box 1397
Buffalo, NY
14240-1397

In Canada
WORLDWIDE LIBRARY
P.O. Box 2800, 5170 Yonge Street
Postal Station A, Willowdale, Ontario
M2N 6J3

Quant.	Title	Price
_____	**WILD CONCERTO,** Anne Mather	$2.95
_____	**A VIOLATION,** Charlotte Lamb	$3.50
_____	**SECRETS,** Sheila Holland	$3.50
_____	**SWEET MEMORIES,** LaVyrle Spencer	$3.50
_____	**FLORA,** Anne Weale	$3.50
_____	**SUMMER'S AWAKENING,** Anne Weale	$3.50
_____	**FINGER PRINTS,** Barbara Delinsky	$3.50
_____	**DREAMWEAVER,** Felicia Gallant/Rebecca Flanders	$3.50
_____	**EYE OF THE STORM,** Maura Seger	$3.50
_____	**HIDDEN IN THE FLAME,** Anne Mather	$3.50
_____	**ECHO OF THUNDER,** Maura Seger	$3.95
_____	**DREAM OF DARKNESS,** Jocelyn Haley	$3.95

	YOUR ORDER TOTAL	$_____
	New York residents add appropriate sales tax	$_____
	Postage and Handling	$___.75
	I enclose	$_____

NAME _____

ADDRESS _____ APT.# _____

CITY _____

STATE/PROV. _____ ZIP/POSTAL CODE _____

WW3R

Take 4 best-selling love stories FREE
Plus get a FREE surprise gift!

Special Limited-Time Offer

Mail to   **Harlequin Reader Service** ®

In the U.S.
2504 West Southern Ave.
Tempe, AZ 85282

In Canada
P.O. Box 2800, Station "A"
5170 Yonge Street
Willowdale, Ontario M2N 6J3

YES! Please send me 4 free Harlequin Temptation® novels and my free surprise gift. Then send me 4 brand-new novels every month as they come off the presses. Bill me at the low price of $1.99 each — a 13% saving off the retail price. There are no shipping, handling or other hidden costs. There is no minimum number of books I must purchase. I can always return a shipment and cancel at any time. Even if I never buy another book from Harlequin, the 4 free novels and the surprise gift are mine to keep forever.

Name _____ (PLEASE PRINT)

Address _____ Apt. No. _____

City _____ State/Prov. _____ Zip/Postal Code _____

This offer is limited to one order per household and not valid to present subscribers. Price is subject to change.

HT–SUB–1